To Derek,
Still the owner of the White Hart

Stealing Home

A NOVEL

Irving Weinman

GW00601400

2004 · JOHN DANIEL & COMPANY
McKINLEYVILLE, CALIFORNIA

Published by John Daniel & Company
A division of Daniel and Daniel, Publishers, Inc.
Post Office Box 2790
McKinleyville, CA 95519
www.danielpublishing.com

LIBRARY OF CONGRESS CATALOGING-IN-PUBLICATION DATA
Weinman, Irving, (date)
  Stealing home : a novel / by Irving Weinman.
    p. cm.
  ISBN 1-880284-72-3 (pbk. : alk. paper)
  1. Americans—Central America—Fiction. 2. Hostility (Psychology)—
Fiction. 3. Central America—Fiction. 4. Male friendship—Fiction.
5. Men—Florida—Fiction. 6. Florida—Fiction. I. Title.
  PS3573.E3963S74 2004
  813'.54—dc21
          2003009975

Stealing Home

to Judith

Stealing Home

The Playoff, 1969

IT'S CLOUDLESS THE SECOND DAY after the storm, dry and cool for late May. Even over the glades, the steam won't rise, and the sky is an entire blue transparency as if it were a dome of glass. In from the Gulf, the gulls crisscross Vernon Groves Field where the ballgame's going on. And over the gulls, way, way up, turkey buzzards hang like specks of dirt.

It's the playoff. Turtle Key, the home team, has tied with South Miami for the South Florida Class B High School Baseball Championship. Sensational for Turtle Key, a place so hedged with everglades, so scraggly, it looks, from planes slanting north towards Naples, not so much a town as bits of driftwood near little piles of red brick. The visitors' stand is solid blue and gold with kids who've bussed across the Tamiami Trail from big suburban South Miami. The home stand is speckled yellow and green, most of it on turtle hats that give their wearers heavy, flat-topped looks. On some, cloth turtleheads bob broken-necked over the visors. What fills the bigger home stands are local adults, not only parents of players, but anyone who can take the afternoon off, which in Turtle Key is almost everyone. Many of the adults segregate themselves so as not to hear the teenagers talk smut nor smell the marijuana that wafts like burnt oregano up from the dark under the stands.

Four of the watching adults aren't locals. They're college scouts, large men in homburgs and wide ties loosened from deep, unbuttoned collars. Two are from Florida State, one is from U. Miami, and the other from Rollins. They're looking over two players. One is the South Miami pitcher, Dan Grosjak. The Turtle Key coach, Harold Jones, feels strange to catch himself admiring the opposing pitcher, but what's he supposed to do? This left-hander reminds him of a young Warren Spahn. Not that his own Ritchie Martinez isn't pitching well, but truth is that if South Miami were batting to form, it wouldn't be a one-all tie here in the bottom of the ninth. And now, one out and no one on, it's Turtle Key's last good chance in regular innings.

A ragged cheering starts, it takes shape: "Yay, Billy. Hey, Billy Rae! Hey! Hey! Billy Rae! Hey! Hey! Billy Rae!" Turtlehead kids are standing, their fists punching heaven with each cheer.

The Rollins scout, a droop-eyed man named John Crombie, sucks an indigestion tab and sees the Miami and FSU scouts set to add notes on Billy Raeburn, the other prospect, up at bat. Crombie's noted enough. It's a farce, his being here. Rollins can't compete against the state's two sports monsters, not for a player of Raeburn's caliber. Only a junior, and it's the second year he's hit over five hundred. And he's fast and a good shortstop, though in the majors they'd probably play him in center or left field. Crombie swallows the minty chalk saliva and wonders why Rollins bothers. Not that he minds watching: this kid's a natural, a budding DiMaggio.

Billy Raeburn drops the weight ring in the on-deck circle and takes a few blur-fast cuts with the bat on his way to the box. He's sixteen and he's six feet tall, with the build of someone matured early. His face, too, has something adult in it, a patient focus, though this is at odds with his almost foolishly good looks—large blue eyes, bowed lips, an uptipped, unformed nose. The girls think he's a doll. A freshman named Mary Ann Jackson has told her best friend Cindy Curry not to tell anyone, but she thinks he's beautiful as a golden Lab puppy and she's going to get him. Now all Mary Ann's girlfriends know and tell her she's crazy. Billy doesn't know her even to say Hi to.

He steps up to the plate and hears a young voice shout, "No pitcher, Billy!" He could almost smile, Mickey Berman is so wrong. He wonders if Mr. Berman, who he works for, is here. Old Higgs must be. He thinks Grosjak is the best pitcher he's ever faced. The way his left arm keeps coming at you like there's this extra joint that whips the ball out after you think he's already let go. He tightens his grip and sees his knuckles stick out swollen, red and blue. The bastard. And his mother. He won't think of them. Even looking at the clear blue sky would get him crazy. It doesn't matter anymore.

The third base coach signals him to take the pitch. He watches the curve sweep in and juts back his hips, but it catches the corner, a strike call. He walks away and looks up at the stands. He doesn't see his mother because she's not there. It doesn't matter. He's done all the looking out for her he's going to. All he wants to do is reach base. All he wants. Not to see the sky break into pieces and the shadows jump up black as hell.

The coach signals to swing away. The infield is back so deep he could bunt. But Billy sees a fastball pour from Grosjak's arm, and he coils tight as it comes waist-high and swings straight across and feels the sweet thunk off the heart of the bat.

Roy Higgs, seeing the ball fly out, jumps to his feet and shakes his big fist. "Yes, goddamnit what a boy, look at that, yessir!" This is the first time he's jumped up all game. He's still plenty strong at fifty-five, but he sees no point in needless jumping. The point here, as he watches the ball fly over the outfield and the left field fence and keep going like it won't come down till Naples, point is that last night over the phone he bet Vern Groves a thousand on Turtle Key. And Higgs is so jumped up he doesn't catch the cheering swallowed into boos or even notice that Billy Raeburn's done a hairpin around first and is trotting back to home plate. When he gets it, he turns to the men both sides of him. "Foul?" he roars. "What in Sam Hill he saying foul? Good goddamn!" He tears off his panama hat; without it he looks taller. Over his green necktie and two-tone brown checked shirt, his bald sun-red head now looks bigger than his belly. The men either side are saying things he doesn't bother to hear.

Roy Higgs sits down wearing the hat and worrying about the nothing-and-two count on Raeburn. Fine boy, athlete the whole town's proud of. But goddamn, nothing and two? Not that he can't afford to drop the thousand. Not that he don't probably have more money than even former U.S. Senator Vernon D. Groves. It's that old Vern's money is a lot older and smoother than his, is why he don't like losing to Turtle Key's favorite son, who is nowadays too fine to live here, even out his own fancy island, comes only for holidays like he was doing them all a favor, instead of owning how this town made him what he is, goddamn it.

Roy is applauding, he's bringing his big red hands together like he was squashing a mosquito. If Billy can't get a hit, nobody can. "Come on, come on, boy!" he calls as if shouting an order. And adds, pleading, "Come on, son!"

Which makes him think of Billy's father. He turns to his right. "Carl, what you say Bob Raeburn was up to? The man should be here for his boy. He knowed I'd a given him the damn day off."

Down on the field, Billy squeezes the rosin bag. He doesn't want to, but he thinks of his father, sees him backing away and thinks bastard, no good prick, and feels terrible. Picking up the bat makes him forget. There's nothing now but now. He steps up, guessing Grosjak will throw another fastball against the odds. When he sees Grosjak shake off two catcher's signals, he's sure.

The ball comes straight down the middle, and into his swing he knows it's a change of pace sinker but he can't check up, and the ball cracks off the underside and bangs hard into the dirt towards third. He's running, letting go the bat, running. The first baseman stretches with his glove out, and Billy brings his head back and thinks of his father yesterday and runs through the bag hearing the ball whack into the glove behind his ear and the umpire's "Sayeeef!"

Roy Higgs is up on his feet again. "You see that? You see how that boy turned a sure out into an infield single? You see that goddamned will power?" On his right, Carl is saying something that Roy can't hear for the cheering. "What you say?" Roy shouts. It's also that Carl has a high and quiet voice. He wears a narrow brimmed brown porkpie and leans his face to Roy's to get heard. It's also that Roy generally turns away from Carl because Carl has teeth missing and the teeth that are there are long and crooked and brown, and Roy would rather not look. But he brings his ear close. "What? What?" Carl says, "Said Bob said he was gonna see maybe he could get them dredgers back over the project."

The project is the heart of Roy Higg's life. Seventy houses from out a damned mangrove swamp. He's making somewheres real of Turtle Key. He sits. The two either side of him sit like all three are toys on a skewer of iron. Roy turns left. "What in hell's wrong with Bob? Those dredgers still being fixed, right?" This other man, Jase, says, "Far as I know, boss." He's losing the smile from Billy Raeburn's single: he'll have to cover butt, if Roy keeps asking. Roy looks at him. "What's Raeburn gonna do with two broke dredgers?" Jase sees his opening, says, "I asked him. Was he crazy or what? He looked in bad shape. Bob said he was some hung over but nothing that wouldn't blow off. Said he was taking a crew to see if the dredgers was fixed enough to tow back, maybe finish them on site." Roy says, "Well, anyways." He's forgetting about Bob now that the winning run is on first, another good hitter, this nigger boy Jeff Rogers, is up, and only one out. Roy can smell the fresh sea air and hamburgers.

Billy knows he has to steal second so that if Jeff gets a hit he can score. But it's a hard steal against the left-hander. At Grosjak's wind-up, he's taken a big lead, crouched, swaying towards second. He sees Grosjak's shoulder open out and he jumps and dives back, his hand on the bag just at the sound of the ball. The first baseman's sweep doesn't touch him. He stands on the base and slowly dusts himself. The first baseman throws back to the pitcher saying, "Nice one, Dan." Then, his back to Billy, he says, "Almost, Raeburn." Billy looks out to second and says, "The throw was good. You weren't." He takes three slow long strides off base and dances forwards and back towards second. He knows it's just him and Grosjak. Despite yesterday, the pleasure of his concentration lights his face. As Grosjak continues his wind-up, Billy sees his shoulder stay high and he takes off for second. The second baseman runs for the base ahead of him. He senses the blur of the ball from the catcher and throws himself head first as if the ground were a wall he dived down. He slams into the fielder and grabs the bag with both hands. He opens his eyes to see the second baseman lift onto one knee and pick up the ball. When Billy stands on second he can hear the cheering. Then he remembers again and the cheers don't matter.

Roy Higgs is up, hat in fist, loving how Billy exploded into second, poor dumb fielder didn't have a chance stretched waiting for the ball, seeing out the corner of his eye Billy come at him like some goddamned guided missile. He says, "Know what Billy Raeburn's got, Jason?"

Jase, smiling again, pulls at the visor of his Higgs Construction cap and says, "Speed."

"Balls. The boy is got balls," Roy says. Roy wishes that Billy was his own son, or, what he means, that if Roy Jr. only had that drive, could just shine some like that. He starts thinking of what he's gonna say to sass Vern Groves when he calls him up Baton Rouge, after Turtle Key wins. Carl is tapping his arm. "Whassit, Carl?"

Carl cups his mouth at Roy's ear. Roy hears "...ain't he wavin at us?"

"Wavin? Damn, here's a couple thousand people wavin all over the place. Who you mean wavin where?"

Carl uncups his mouth and yells quietly in Roy's face, "Smiley Green, down front the right field bleachers, makin for us, see?"

Roy looks for a black face. Not so many niggers he can't find Smiley. He sees him and waves, asks, "Why wouldn't Bob Raeburn have Smiley his crew chief?" And before Carl or Jase can answer, he makes out the oily shine of Smiley's work clothes. "Better get down there, Carl, see what he wants." Always something, Roy thinks. Give them the damned day off, they still find something he's got to fix.

Now on Grosjak's blind side, Billy walks casually off second. The fielder backs off. Grosjak looks but won't try anything. Billy shakes a little more toward third, hoping to spook the infielders and catcher. Grosjak turns, pitches, and Jeff hits it in the air. Billy sees it dropping towards the gap in right-center and takes off, but the third base coach is waving him back. He turns near third to see the right fielder getting to his feet with the ball in his glove. He sprints back and slides into second as the throw comes in wide. He gets up on the base and dusts off, angry, sweat running down his forehead. If he'd waited, he could have tagged up and been on third. He looks at his knuckles swollen from yesterday and starts to remember. He won't look at the sky. She should be here, at least stand up to the bastard that much. But forget it: he has to get to third.

Roy Higgs is blaming himself. Counting his chickens too soon like some dumb cluck. He's not listening to Jason commiserating. Jason don't have a thousand riding on this. Two outs and Billy, good as he is, stuck on second. Roy is thinking of some old Baton Rouge plantation house and Vern—no, be Senator Groves up there—and his oil buddies, and Vern saying something as to how he just won a thousand off some down-home cracker with more money than brains... The hamburger smell gets up his nose again and Roy's real hungry, could do justice to a couple them burgers. He stands as Carl comes back up. He'll send him down for food. "Well, Smiley want something?" Carl looks glum, but, shit, Carl always looks glum.

Carl's taking off his porkpie and looking at it. "Yessir, Roy. Thing is, is Bob Raeburn he got killed. Towing cable snapped and the end whipped his head. Smiley said he kept warning Bob, but Bob wouldn't slow down. Smiley just came from the hospital, said no one saw how Bob could be alive, though the hospital ain't said nothin final. They called Emily. She's over with Bob. With the body, I guess."

Jase stands, says, "Who's gonna tell Billy?"

Roy cannot believe this bad luck, sky's so damned blue. He says, "Let's just sit down and calm down. I'm gonna tell him, Goddamn, who in hell else suppose to tell him. You? Smiley? Whisperin Carl, here?"

Out at second, Billy hears the heart go out of the cheers. It doesn't matter because it's all gone now. He means it's just him. It was always going to be. He has to steal home. He'll make third because Grosjak will concentrate on striking Sawyer out. And he will, three straight pitches, probably. So he has two pitches to get from second to home. He looks up at the sky so hard he squeezes the blue right out of it. Then he walks five paces off second, catches the third baseman's eye and gives him a little nod. The third baseman backs towards the bag.

Roy Higgs is watching the Sawyer kid try to shake his nerves off as he comes to the plate. He wonders how bad it is to still be interested in the ballgame what with Bob Raeburn dead. Poor bastard. A drinker, not the easiest sort, but a damned good foreman, good old boy. Roy sighs. He'll see them right, Emily and Billy. The daughter's already married so that's... Will his Workman's Comp pay up? Inspectors might say no because of the rough water and dredgers still under repair shouldn't have been out. Shit.

Jase says, "Poor kid. Roy, you don't think maybe Billy should be told, like now?"

Roy turns: "That's some fine goddamn idea, Jason. Boy's got maybe three minutes more of feeling fine for years, you want to take that away. Praise God you don't have kids. Anyhow, how? I supposed to run down get Harold to stop the goddamned game? Or was it pulling Billy off second for a slower pinch-runner you maybe had in mind?"

"You're right, Roy. Dumb idea, sorry." Carl leans in and says across Roy, "You some peckerhead, Jase." Roy thinks Jason maybe couldn't hear Carl and says, "He says you're a peckerhead."

Billy knows Grosjak won't bother with a pitchout. He could throw underhand and strike out Sawyer. Grosjak glances back in his wind-up and then looks forward, and Billy's off, hearing nothing but the thud of his feet and seeing the third baseman stretching for the ball which won't be thrown. The coach signals not to bother to slide. A bump off Billy's hip as he runs through the base. He turns in the cheering to see the third baseman getting up off the ground. Dirkson the third base coach is patting his back. "Way to run, Billy!"

"Tough guy," the third baseman without the ball says. Billy stands on the bag, leans into the third baseman and says, "Tough shit." The third baseman trots into the pitcher to quiet his own nerves. Everyone's jumpy now. The pitch was a ball, and that's all

19

the luck he can expect. A seagull swoops over the infield. He thinks its wings are knives slicing the solid blue.

Carl, in the stands, stares down feeling low for Billy and sorry for Roy having to tell him about his pa. He says, "Seems special hard, I mean it being such a good game and all." Roy, for a change, hears him. "You mean what, a good game is worst than a bad one would be?" "Aw, you know what I mean. No need to jump down my throat."

No need, Roy thinks, for him to be sitting between two peckerheads, neither. It's good Billy's having a good game, help get him an FSU scholarship. He wonders how to break the news. All at once, or bit by bit: his dad's been in an accident, a bad accident, as bad an accident as can be. Shit, no, that'd be a kind of torture. How would his own son want to be told if it was him dead? Roy fiddles with the doohickey back of his tie that the back part's supposed to slide into and tries to imagine Roy Jr. among all his fancy friends up Chapel Hill. Not that he's not proud of him, but to have a son like Billy... He figures Roy Jr. wouldn't mind how he was told, long as it didn't embarrass him in that fraternity of his. Wouldn't want to own his pa was a hard-working redneck. No, sir. Not for a member of Si, Pi, Pss...whatever in hell its Greek letters was. You'd think the American alphabet had plenty enough good letters to name some damn North Carolina boy's club.

Billy on third isn't listening to coach Dirkson. He's looking at the catcher, figuring he's good but skinny, so he'll have to run into him so he won't have time to get set solid. The crowd knows now. They're calling out what's on his mind. The whole home crowd is up on their feet shouting, "Steal home! Steal home!" Like his own breathing. Kids with hats like turtles. Disappearing into shells, fading away like she did. His mother should be here. No sky now. All right, just him and home plate.

Sawyer better not swing and foul. Billy takes his lead down the third base line and Grosjak pitches so fast that he just thinks

NO and runs back to third. A strike. The catcher comes forward holding the ball, calming the infield. He looks over to Billy and then throws the ball back to Grosjak. And now Billy sees how to do it.

He sidesteps down the line again as Grosjak winds up. He takes an extra step and Grosjak throws a curve strike two. Billy turns back towards third, head over his shoulder. As the catcher moves up and commits to throw, Billy pivots and takes off for home. Grosjak is startled as he waits for the ball, and Billy's halfway down the line running. In the crowd's roar, his roar, running. The catcher turns, running back to take Grosjak's throw high, reaching up and spinning for home plate behind him. Everything is Billy running, launching himself, legs bucked up and kicking out, feeling the earth, the plate, the catcher's arms against his cleats. Screaming, dust in his mouth, hearing the screaming. He slits open his eyes to see the catcher four feet back from him, mitt up with the ball in it. Out, he's out. The umpire throwing down his mask: "Don't you swear at me, son! You dropped the ball and put it back when you rolled over. The runner's safe. Safe!" He sweeps out a big two-handed safe sign and walks off. "And that's the ballgame!" he calls back. And the yelling is covering everything. Everyone's all over him, pounding, pulling, lifting him up, and it doesn't matter now. Now is already gone.

He fights them off, pushes away. Shouts of "Givim room" and "Back off, there." He shrugs and elbows blind through the home-plate crowd and bumps into Grosjak. They nod at each other in the yelling. They shake hands, Billy says, "You had me on that sinker. I was lucky to catch any of it." Grosjak talks at his ear: "Where you gonna take, Billy? Miami or FSU? I'm going for FSU." "Guess I will, too. Don't know. Still a year to go." He wishes he could smile at Grosjak, or something. Grosjak says, "Maybe see you on the same team. Good luck." Billy says, "Sure." Coach Jones is coming at him shouting. "Stealing home!" A hand thumps his shoulder and turns him. Mr. Higgs with two of the men. Billy has to say something. "Thanks a lot, Mr. Higgs." He realizes Higgs hasn't said anything yet.

Roy Higgs keeps hold of Billy's shoulder and shakes hands with him. The boy seems to wince. "No," Roy says. "Great game, Billy."

"Thanks, sir."

"No, I mean, Billy, I've got some bad news." He sees Billy nodding like he hasn't heard him, so he speaks loud and slow. "I mean bad as news can be. Your father. There's been an accident and your father's been, he died, son." Roy starts to put his hand on Billy's other shoulder to hug the boy in.

"Thanks, Mr. Higgs."

"No, Billy!" Roy shouts. It must be all this crowd yelling. He motions Carl and Jason and the three of them draw Billy a little away. Jason goes over to tell Coach Harold Jones.

Billy understands he hasn't heard. Higgs isn't congratulating him. "Sorry, I didn't get you."

"Billy, son, your dad died in an accident. I'm real sorry, truly I am sorry." Now Roy sees that Billy's heard, and he pulls the boy into him. He can smell the sweat and earth from Billy's steal and wishes he had a son like him. Also he is sorry as hell for old Bob and for Billy, but he can' help remembering the thousand he's just won off Vern Groves.

"Dead," Billy says.

"Yes," Roy says. He pats Billy's back. Grit comes off onto his hand. "It's very hard. But you have to take it like a man, boy."

"My father's dead."

"I'm surely sorry. Your Ma's over to the hospital, where he is. We'll take you right over. And don't you worry none, I'm gonna look after you and your ma. That's a promise."

Billy is saying something Roy can't hear. "What?"

He's saying, "I knew it. I knew he'd die." His knuckles hurt like yesterday. He stares out over Higg's checked shirt, past the unfinished night-light poles. There's a gap there in the fence through which he can see out to the Gulf, to the horizon, to the line of the vanishing flat planes where he really is.

I. Sunshine

Chapter One _____

I'M NOT SURE WHY Bill Raeburn was a hero. Even now, with his whole life there to look back on, there's something I don't get, or can't name. Nor could he; of course, the hero these days isn't supposed to know he's one. He needs to be the John Wayne or Jimmy Stewart—Aw, shucks—hero, not the classical hero who precisely knows his worth. Anyway, who am I, Mickey Berman, to know what is and isn't heroic? I'm a local pianist with a little too much money to need to work. What I know is that Bill Raeburn was an ex-ballplayer who failed to live up to his promise, a failed businessman, and a failed husband and father, and yet he was a hero, became one that summer we lost him, those months that burned holes in everyone's heads, regardless of hats or parasols, too hot even for our town, Turtle Key, whose usual steam bath days seemed like cool mists in that summer of 1993.

The heat had arrived in May, but that summer, Bill's summer, began for me the June day Anita Groves showed up in town. Anita

Higgs as she was then and is now. I'd gotten up early to beat the worst of the heat. It was just after dawn, and Ginny was already out of bed.

I made coffee and went out onto the roof. Ginny was at the parapet. I asked what she thought of the view.

"Too many churches."

I put my arm around her shoulders. Before us rose the high stiletto spire of Our Lady Queen of the Sea and the Episcopal battlements of St. George's. And beyond them were the lower spires of lower churches, and, somewhere beneath them all, the synagogue my father had helped found, an extended bungalow. I was trying to decide if Ginny was smart.

I said, "You can see the gulf." I was trying to sell the view. The gulf was smooth, a cream-blue silk stretched tight under the boats.

"Hey, you can see that anywhere in Florida. How can you stand living in such a cracker town?"

My hand dropped off her shoulder. She took it and placed it on her ass. Ginny was short. She had bright black eyes which gave nothing away.

I told her, "You sound like my father's Philly and Miami relatives. In '46 they warned him not to come out here. They called it the *Goyishe* Gulf."

"They were right."

"My father was happy and successful."

"Successful and happy," she corrected. "He had jewelry stores up and down the coast. You just sit in this dump when you could play anywhere—Miami, even New York."

I sang in a rough blues voice: "I done wandered, baby. But now my wanderin's done done." We walked out of the sun and sat under the awning. I poured coffee. I said, "You may be right; I may have become a Jewish cracker, a matzo. On the other hand, I'm part owner of the club I play in." Then I threw back my head and yodeled: "Home, home on the roof. Where Manischevitz is ninety-six proof."

Ginny smiled, "Don't get me wrong, lover. The penthouse and roof garden are great."

Her compliment made me nervous. This had been my father's original store, The Samuel Berman Building, three-story, late Art Deco, the tallest building in town, not counting church spires and aerials. I said, "I don't think Sam would like it much these days, all pink, with its eyebrows and trim a demented magenta, like a ten-year-old kid gone bananas with her mother's makeup."

She looked confused. Was it rejecting her compliment? Or didn't she know what an eyebrow was? I smiled to hide my embarrassment. Ginny Gordon was an old girlfriend who once a year ran away from her Miami lawyer husband, Howard. She'd drive across the Everglades and turn up at the club late and spend a night or two. She had a lively, affectionate tush. "So are you going to stay some, my old flame?"

"I can't. I have to get up to my sister's in Fort Meyers this morning."

She'd said this before. I had the idea the sister could be another old boyfriend, but that wasn't my problem. The song went: *My old flame, I can't remember her name...* "If you stayed a little longer, you might get to like the place." I was flirting out of habit, already imagining how we'd close our eyes when we kissed goodbye.

"What's to like? And if it's so great, how come you spent all those years after college up in New York?"

"Playing music, listening, learning music. Not that I worked all the time. No, Sam supported me. Those were good years for him. He'd say, 'Van Cleef and Arpels I'm not, but I'm doing okay, thank you.' And I was the only child, the darling boy. He even tried to understand jazz for my sake but figured he was too old. He said it seemed as rich and complicated as classical music. He said—I remember his words—'You've got to respect an art form practiced by someone named Thelonius Monk. A name, it's better than Van Cleef and Arpels, it's as good as Savanarola.'"

Ginny said, "I don't get it."

I shouldn't have told her. I said, "Savanarola was an Italian monk, a renaissance monk."

She punched my arm. "That's what I mean. Italian monks, renaissance: who can you talk with here about things like that?"

I thought, not you, for one. "You'd be surprised," I said. "And then when Sam died, I thought I might come back and stick around. But those same damned relatives, the ones who told him never to come here: they were so used to envying my father's success that they looked forward to me inheriting their displeasure." I didn't care if Ginny could or couldn't understand this; I was essentially retelling the story to myself. I stood and went to a big tub of areca palms. "The funeral, my god. I hated the way they eyed me over their plates of chopped liver. They said, almost in chorus, 'So now you'll stop the piano and take over the business?' What they meant was stop the jazz, the *horrible schvartze noise*. Bunch of creeps. Two weeks later, I'd pretty well sold the business, the houses, everything except this building, and went back to a gig in New York."

"But you didn't stay."

I moved behind the palms and put my head through: "It was a jungle. It took me three years to get out." Here, despite the props, my story was bullshit, because I'd left out its central character, El Señor Cocaine.

"But why here, Mickey? Why this jerk town?"

I came back around the palms. "You're right, the views are nothing special for south Florida." I opened my arms in benediction over the town: "But blessed are the seedy sites, for they shall inherit less tourists, less franchises, less *chazerai*." I turned to Ginny with my arms still up, feeling my robe slip open. "Besides, I like it that everyone knows everyone, and I like the transparency of the place, how even its corruption is unhidden. It's like someone with psoriasis who won't go around in long sleeves because it's too damned hot."

Ginny was laughing, clapping her hands. Did she know the meaning of psoriasis? Of Thelonius?

"Oh, lover, look at you all undone and well hung."

Her amusement made me jumpy. I wanted to play the piano or vacuum the penthouse. I said, "We have time to go back to bed before you leave." Politeness.

She came into my robe and squeezed me. "I like your bed. I like how you kid yourself, just like I do."

"Baby love, that's heavy for seven in the deep south morning and you a woman on the run and me only your midnight man." But I thought Ginny wasn't so dumb. We went to bed, but nothing much happened, as I guess we both might have predicted. Three hours later, I'd said goodbye and was at the piano, trying to work some ironic dissonance behind the first three notes of *I Married an Angel*. My father married an angel, because Celia was pretty and mothers had to be angels. Bill Raeburn had, because Mary Ann was sweet and friend's wives had to be angels. What I had married were liaisons and one night stands and—what to call this thing with Ginny—occasional, half understandings?

By late morning, I felt too stressed to stay home. I thought I'd work at the song on the sharper, dryer piano at the club. The club: on inheriting Meyer's estate, I'd put some money into Frank Edrich's idea for a club, which, these ten years later, made me its junior partner. I had a trio there, and took home some profit, and mostly lay low after New York and the clinic, which is to say after vacuuming much money up my fine Jewish nose. Ginny wasn't dumb, nor was I kidding myself, too much, about why I was here.

The Sponger's Club was only six blocks away, but I put the top down on the Caddy and drove. My father bought the car new in '69 and kept it for me to learn to drive on. After Sam's death, I garaged it on blocks, and when I returned, I put it back on the road. It had a powder blue body and white leather upholstery. It was like driving a sofa. More: sitting in it, I could imagine the smell of Sam's illegal Havanas mixed with the smell of canvas, chrome, and saddle soap. I turned onto North Wharf Street and, as if answering Ginny's question, sang: *Momma may have, and Poppa may have, but God bless the child who's got his own.*

Church bells were clanging noon when I parked on the dock and went into the Sponger's Club. It was named for the old sponge sheds from which it had been converted, single story wooden buildings with high pitched tin roofs up on Dade pine rafters. Under the stale of the smoke and drink, they still held the briny smell of iodine. I gave my usual nod hello to Mr. Sponger over the bar. This was a sponge-stuffed effigy in top hat and tails, clothes that had once been Sam's. All I'd done was contribute the clothes. Frank had a New Orleans carnival mask maker construct it, and no one but I saw in it a resemblance to Sam or could appreciate its ironies. In life, my father had never been drunk and was proud of never having borrowed a nickel. And here he was Mr. Sponger, the boozer epitome (Sam's despised *schicker*) and quintessential cadger (Sam's despised *schnorer*)—the sponger, the total soak.

Actually, Bill Raeburn sensed the resemblance, too, despite the face of sponge and dark glasses and pasted-on moustache and goatee. When he first saw the effigy he said he didn't know whether to ask for a beer or a tray of engagement rings.

Terrence was setting up behind the bar. He was chief bartender and bouncer, black muscles rippling from out a sharp Hawaiian shirt.

"Terrence."

"Mickey. You're in early."

"I need to work at the piano. Is Frank in?"

"Not yet. I saw Cal Joe this morning. He asked after you. And she did, down there." Terrence gave one of those sideways nods without looking, the kind that only bartenders behind bars can give.

I turned and saw a beautiful blond. Then I recognized Anita Higgs, and she didn't seem so knockout. It was some censorship at work about her being Senator Groves daughter, all that position and money, the onetime princess of Turtle Key, now its empress, though mostly *in absentia*. I went smiling to the end of the bar. "Anita." Heavy lips and honey hair and fourteen hundred dollar sunglasses.

"Hey, Mickey. Mickey!"

We hugged. I felt I'd never liked her. "What are you doing here?"

"A vodka and grapefruit," she said.

"Big city funny. I didn't know you were in town. Nothing in the TK *Citizen*."

She took off her glasses. She had large gray eyes that jumped around a bit too much. She said, "We're on one of Roy's sentimental business visits. He gets to pretend he's a good ole boy and I get... Listen, yesterday I was supposed to give an impromptu talk to the Women's Club, 'Living in Our Nation's Capital.' Roy's idea. Can you imagine? I couldn't. I didn't go and Roy was burnt."

I wasn't fascinated with this glimpse into the lives of the rich and bored. "How long are you going to be in town?"

"A few weeks. Then we're off to Mayan ruins and hummingbirds in the Yucatan and Guatemala."

"Maybe you and Roy could drop in one night before you go."

"Me with Roy? You know what Roy's reaction to my not going to that awful Women's Club was?"

I shrugged and picked up her sunglasses. The frames were a tiny checkerwork of shell or mineral, like two-tone butterscotch.

She put her hand on mine. "You know, you're one of the only people here I can talk to. You still have beautiful hands. Wasn't it me who nicknamed you Fingers, back in high school? Fingers Berman."

"No, it wasn't you. Besides, the rest of us were back in high school. You were wherever, Miss Wasp's Finishing School. I remember me and my high school trio hired to play out on the island for your sweet sixteen party."

"Was I really such a snob?"

"No, maybe not."

"Wait a second, didn't I put out for you?"

"You were drunk and we kissed."

"Not true, I'm not coming on, but, in the interest of historical accuracy, you felt my tits."

I looked at her red silk shirt and laughed. "Okay, okay. I copped a feel off you in 1974 and I can't deny it. It'll be on my gravestone. Like: Say he was no leader, no great healer, But say one night Anita let him feel her. Up."

"Oh, that's good. That's 'Jenny Kissed Me.' What do you *do* with yourself in this swamp-life town?"

"You're the second person who's asked me that today. Let me get you a drink." I wanted a whiskey but asked for a club soda. Terrence smiled approval, though he knew whiskey was a better habit than the one it replaced.

"Okay, so what was Roy's reaction to your revolt?"

"It was one of Roy's elaborate little jokes. You remember Carl, Roy Sr.'s gofer? That man makes a redneck look like a courtier at Versailles. Well, Roy has Carl gardening at the Island; that is, sitting on a tractor mower doing nothing, but doing it noisily, all day. So Roy is burnt and I apologize for not going, after I promised to, and I ask him can I make him some lunch. We're out at the swimming pool. And he says no. He guesses he'll have Carl make him a cold pork sandwich, like he used to. So I say, Oh, sure, because, what, you really like the way it comes with Carl's greasy thumbprint in the white bread? And Roy calls Carl over. Carl, you understand, looks like he's just come from his morning bath in an oil sump, and Roy asks him to make him a cold pork sandwich on white bread with lots of mayonnaise. So Carl says, Sure Roy. If Roy said, Carl, would you please decapitate Mrs. Higgs, here, Carl'd say, Sure, Roy. Then Carl says he'll just go up and wash his hands, and Roy looks at me and says, No, Carl, like that'd be just fine. At which I decide I've stuck around for enough bubba comedy and go up to the house to change. Half an hour later I come back down to the pool. Carl is chugging off on the mower and Roy is sitting at the table sipping a beer. And there is this sandwich with a filthy thumbprint pressed in each half. I say, Lovely, a Carl special. Roy says, No, Carl brought this to me perfectly clean. I say, Very funny. He says, Really, I knew you'd be disappointed, so I went over to that tub with the kumquat tree, stuck my thumbs in the dirt and squeezed the sandwiches. I said, That's really hilarious, Roy. He said, No, I mean it. Carl witnessed it. I'll get him. And then, this was what really made me mad, he calls Carl back and Carl comes back, turns off the tractor and slowly comes over, never once looking at me. And then Roy repeats what he told me he did and asks Carl if that was so, and Carl says, Yup, Roy, that's exactly what you done. And then Roy says, Tell Miss Anita, Carl. And Carl repeats, Yes, Miss Nita, that's exactly what Roy done. He said this looking straight into my cleavage. So I said, Ha, ha, Roy. You and *haute cuisine* Carl, here, are very droll. I was talking as if Carl wasn't there, I was so angry."

"And then?"

"I left, promising Roy I'd get even."

"How?"

Anita took a long drink of her vodka and grapefruit, looking at me. Then she shrugged.

I could see how she'd been insulted, but I still thought her

35

reaction was over the top. And I didn't really have anything against Roy, other than he was a pretty thoughtless developer. But then, it's not as if there are really *thoughtful* developers, are there. Especially in Florida. So why did I jump right in? Maybe because it seemed easier to humor her. Maybe because I was looking at her lush red lips and tight red shirt. Anyhow, remembering that Roy was a lobbyist for Coastal Oil—a job he'd been given by Anita's father—I told her she could join SPOIL. And when she said, "What?" I said it was the protest group against oil exploration that Mary Ann and Kate Raeburn belonged to. Perhaps if I hadn't said it or mentioned the Raeburns, Bill wouldn't have become so caught up. At the time, though, it seemed just a bit of bar chat, and I didn't really think she'd give it another thought. But Anita just looked at me with a smile and said, "Maybe I just will, among other things."

After she left, I got to the piano and started working on "I Married an Angel." After an hour, I couldn't make anything happen and decided there were some tunes so inherently square and sentimental it was best to stay away from them.

Chapter Two _____

RAEBURN PARKS, CLOSES HIS EYES and immediately dreams. The sea lies in shiny blue disjointed slabs, like blocks of cracked watercolor. Static and turbulent, they are heaped to a sky not above it but back beyond, an orange sky rising flat from the horizon in a bad imitation of fire.

He opens his eyes. Orange was the sun through his eyelids. He opens the door but can't get out. He sits head down, swallowing against the tequila heartburn. Gray palms against pink. He squeezes his closed eyes to refocus. Black palms against tan: his sports shirt.

He gets out and walks to the other side of the pickup and sees a big heap of blue and orange boxes. He walks towards it slowly, as if his deliberation could make it go away.

What gets him is how it isn't on the loading platform, not even on pallets, not even stacked. Still, if they are not the same, if they are different because this time there are more of them. Way, way too many, but at least if they're the right anchors.

He looks into the sky before he reads the label. The sky is neither blue nor orange. It is colorless and of course they won't be right. He reads with a hard smile: AMERICAN GRABBER 8 LB SPECIAL FOR GRAVEL/STONE BOTTOM.

Yes, certainly. What did he expect? Two months after he returns the shipment of wrong anchors, they ship them back again. More. "Lots more," he says, and continues out loud: "and not a gravel or stone bottom for six hundred miles, of course. Kate. Kate? Kate! Get out here right now, Kate!"

It isn't that he can't hear himself yelling in his parking lot empty of customers' cars. He hears and sees his stupidity beside this hill of useless anchors even as he keeps bellowing "Kate! Kate!" like the horn buoy off Mexican Shoals.

Kate comes running out the back door. "Sorry, Dad. I know."

He sees his hand is held out stiffly towards the pile as if this were an old fashioned opera. He cannot speak. It is all he can do to keep from singing Kate's name, a warning to himself, as she stands before him frowning in anticipation.

"Dad, see, this guy just drove in in this humongous truck and showed me the bills of lading and I knew you were expecting anchors."

She might as well have signed for a truckload of snowshoes. "Didn't you think," he begins, low.

"And you weren't around. Where were you for so long?"

He has been in the Red Parrot, after the bank, understandably. But she is not going to sidetrack him. "You could have called your mother."

"I did. She wasn't home."

Raeburn is trying to be fair to his daughter. He regards the boxes. And the sky, which has now returned to its ordinary, pretty blue, now that the worst has been done. "Couldn't you, didn't you remember the mess about this from two months ago?"

"Sort of, but I was still in school then, I was only working part time."

"Okay, right, true." His operatic hand finally falls to a box top. "But didn't you check the papers?"

"I did, but—"

"Wait. And didn't you see they were for gravel or stone bottoms? Didn't you read the boxes, at least?"

"Dad—"

"And aren't you our big environmentalist? Who has spent most of her seventeen years in and around these waters, our environment, so that you must know there's no gravel or rock here, just sand? And of course coral which you are the first to tell everyone shouldn't be anchored on?" He can hear himself get louder.

"But, Jesus—"

"Don't Jesus me. These are rounded anchors. Made to shovel under rocks and gravel. Not pointed to dig in and hold in the sand. You know? Do you know?" He turns away as if from his own yelling. Then he turns back.

Her arms are folded, her face flushed, glaring.

"Well?" He believes he is quieter. Reasonable.

"Well, if you're finished. If I can say something?"

He gives a deep mock bow. His knuckles whack back into a box.

"This driver, I told him I didn't think so, after I tried to call Mom? But he kept showing me the papers and the order number and your name, so finally I signed it. I mean and he kept saying how he'd driven down all the way from Atlanta."

She was seventeen and bright and careful. She should have known. He says, "But why didn't you check, actually go out and take a look?" At his side, he opens and closes his fist. Kate glances at it.

She says, "I did. That's what I'm trying to tell you. I figured, after I'd signed, that maybe I screwed up, so I went out to the truck and saw they couldn't be right—I mean, I do actually know what the Gulf bottom's like here—and I told him he had to take them back."

"But you'd given him his copy of the bill you'd signed."

"Yes, so he said yes, he'd take them back, and I had to get back into the store for customers because I was alone here. So you know how you can't see or hear back out here when you're at the front counter?"

"Yes, I do. And," he continues, seeing the mean little smile on the driver's face as he did it, "he was mad and had the signed bill—since you didn't have the sense to get it back from him to cross out your signature which is the proof you took delivery—so he just dumped the boxes here."

"Yes, I guess so. I'm sorry."

"Didn't off-load them onto the platform."

"I know."

She knows and he can't stop. "Didn't even leave them on pallets, didn't even leave them stacked."

Kate is looking around at her feet now, embarrassed by his carrying on. He is embarrassed, too, but cannot stop. "He just dumped them off the back of the truck. No, dumped wouldn't be so messy. This has been worked on, the rotten man put some effort into creating this, this…" The word "disarray" comes to his mind, but in the operatic context is so like a bad translation from Italian that Raeburn can only repeat "this, this."

"This," walking half around the giant pile. "This," his hand jerking out toward the orange and blue mound and then recoiling back as if it burned, some theatrical stove of fate turned on.

She says, "Please just go inside. It's my fault. I'll stack them on the platform."

And just when he thinks she's a selfish brat, she comes up with this. If she were a son he could say, Damn right it's your fault, and walk away and feel better. Instead she's paying for Charlie Styles warning about the loan repayments and then his hour at the Parrot where he drank, though he was no drinker, though the two tequilas and beers have given him nothing but a headache, a heartburn, and a banged hand.

He says in lower voice, "I knew you couldn't be left in charge. I'll get these later." He knows he shouldn't have said this, but he's afraid if he starts apologizing he might burst out yelling and make her feel worse, and he wants this summer before she leaves home for college to be nice for her.

"Anyhow," she says, in step with him, "you won't pay for them until they give us the right ones."

"That's exactly right." He thinks to put his arm around her shoulder, but they're at the door and, as he opens it, he remembers he's actually paid for the first wrong load of anchors. Off Kate's red-blond hair as she passes him, comes the smell of strawberry shampoo. It occurs to Raeburn in the impossible pink hopefulness of this smell that he is not going to be able to pay for his daughter to go to college. As he has promised her and her mother and himself.

He says, "You tend the store, I'll be in the office. Any sales?"

"I sold the four-seater LeBeq."

"That's good. Not an out-of-town check?"

"Come on. The guy's credit card went through."

"Well, I thought we'd never move it."

She nods. He watches her go up front. Maybe it's not as bad as he'd thought. There's always the Higgs underwriting. Maybe not always, Roy Junior not being who his father was. Roy has no responsibility for Old Roy's promise. And that was made because of that playoff game as much as for what he'd thought was his father's death, which turned out to be his father's early senility or whatever that religious mania was called.

He sits at his desk, straightens the already straightened papers and calls Higgs Holdings and gets put right through to Roy.

"Roy, Bill Raeburn. Heard you were in town. How're you doing?"

"Why just fine Bill. Got in a few days ago. Can't stay away from home too long. How you doin, Bill?"

"Okay, fine. Charlie Styles at First Southern told me I

shouldn't count on you, on Higgs Holdings, as guarantor of my loan much longer. Is that so?"

"I don't know, I don't get to see… Oh, yes, someone showed me some pretty discouraging figures: interest payments not met, something like doubling the debt in six quarters. Six quarters, was it?"

"Yes."

"Some three hundred thousand plus dollars?"

It is three hundred and thirty-six thousand and six hundred and forty-two, as of a few hours ago at the bank. By now it will be more. Raeburn remembers a sign in New York City with the national debt on it and as you watch it keeps spinning up dollars, tens, thousands, tens of thousands, faster than your eye can take in. Or is that the sign with the acres of rain forest destroyed, or with the number of gun deaths as you watch?

"I know it's bad, Roy. It's not just the recession but also all I've lost to the downtown marina. I took the loan to expand this one at your company's urging. Then you build that downtown marina with its own marine supply store. Bang goes my business as well as my marina plans." Raeburn is angry as much for having to say this to Roy; it sounds pathetic, wheedley.

"Look, ole buddy, I try to honor my daddy's wishes, and I'm not going to pull the plug on you tomorrow, but you were never more than a hundred thousand in the hole to him. And I know you think well, shoot, what's three hundred thousand to someone has the biggest development business in southwest Florida, but, hey, you gotta look after the pennies, you want the pounds to take care of themselves."

He hears Roy's voice go pinchy, like in those comic strips where people put clothespins on their noses. His hands are lining up the lined-up papers. The difference between him and Roy is his pennies are pennies; Roy's are hundreds of thousands of dollars. He says, "I've never thought you were bound by any of Old Roy's arrangements with me."

"I know. Just do my accountants the favor of getting on the repayment wagon again, is all I'm askin. Oh, and somethin personal: I don't want to interfere in your family life none, but do Mary Ann and Kate really have to be right in the middle of that anti-oil protest bunch? Not that they gonna do anythin serious, but it's kinda embarrassin, me an oil lobbyist an we all bein ole friends an such."

"I'll get paying the bank again by the next payment date. As for the other, you're right. It's nothing you should interfere in. I'll see you around."

"Hey, no offense meant, bubba. You take care now."

He puts down the phone finding everything about the call offensive: the phony home-town buddiness, Roy's studied bad grammar, the word "bubba" out of Roy's mouth greasy as an oil bubble.

He puts it from his mind: he does the calculation on a pad of paper. Debt times interest points divided by four. There it is, twelve thousand six hundred in under three months. If he has a good season. He would have an okay season but for Roy Higgs' new downtown marina. And the house mortgaged twice in that great expansion plan seven years ago, which he has come to think of as those crippling good times. And no bank in the state going to loan him a penny—a three hundred thousand dollar unit to Roy—with his outstanding debt and debt repayment record. He imagines another banker, like Mitch Harris at Atlantic Federal, asking why he just doesn't get some further underwriting from Higgs Holdings.

He can hear Mary Ann, too, warning him not to put all his eggs in Roy Higgs' basket. And his own voice pointing out there was no other basket to carry them.

Raeburn listens in the hum of the office a/c. That could be an economy. He could shut the air conditioning when he wasn't in the office. Keep it off all the time, work happy as a sand flea in hundred and three degrees. And who in hell did Roy think he was, telling him what Mary Ann and Kate should or shouldn't think of oil exploration.

He leaves his office, walks up the passage to where he can see into the store, Kate with a customer, a kid in a T-shirt. Not much of a customer there, not someone who's looking for a few hundred anchors for small boats in Maine.

Raeburn goes back into his office. His hand moves across the stacked papers on his desk, gently mussing them like he might his wife or daughter's hair. Twelve six. He can sell his boat. Worth eighteen but he won't get more than seven five. Motors alone worth twelve. His sister has nothing to lend him. Mickey, but he won't ask. Might as well leave the town now, sell up everything if he starts begging off friends.

He sees the papers spread all over his desk. *His* desk? What is his now? When has it ever been? He leans against the pine paneling. A stillness comes over him, like a stone dropped in deep water.

It is difficult to move his cheek off the pine, it feels so heavy. His shoulder drops, his weight rocks back and he swings in behind his fist and smashes the wall.

The paneling is not even cracked, it is that thick, the wood that good. The cheap paneling of his old office had been antiqued with the splints and dents of his fists. His stone cheeks lift in a smile. That good, the whole first class refurbishing and expansion six years before that was going to turn everything around. Rather than what it has done—eat all the profits in his dream of profit. Pine paneling, the central a/c, new shop fittings, enlarged warehousing (Mr. Raeburn, they'll buy more if it's here in front of them). The posts he's sunk for marina dockage. He's sunk. The upstairs space he uses for working out that was built as the watchman's apartment. A live-in night watchman! Dreams. Crap. He has had to let Mike go who has worked hard for him for ten years. Something he must ask Kate. Now there is only him and Mary Ann and today Kate.

He shouts, "Kate!" The knuckles on two fingers are bloody, swelling up. He licks them as he walks up the passage. "Kate!"

Two men are leaving. Kate puts down a receipt book. "Just sold two of the good life jackets and eight flotation cushions."

He nods. If they sold a hundred of the good life jackets and ten LeBeq inflatables a day, it wouldn't be enough. He says, taking care not to shout, "What exactly do you and your mother do in that anti-oil group?"

"It's not anti-oil, it's against any further oil exploration down here in the Gulf."

"Right, but what do you do here in Turtle Key?"

"Well, it's linked to other similar groups along the Gulf coast. And, you know, we try to educate people to the facts, like how little potential oil reserve is down here compared to the big environmental risks of pipeline spills and tanker spills, like up at Fort Meyers? We want to stop the oil business from ruining the Gulf water, the fish, and the birds, and the sea grasses. Come on, you understand, the ecology. So we hold protests and issue press releases and give talks at schools, and like that. Do you want to join? That would be great."

He looks at his daughter.

She says, "No, I guess not, what with Mr. Higgs being an oil lobbyist, and everything. I can understand how you feel. It's a free country."

She understands how he feels. He imagines not having his boat, not getting out on the ocean, out to the islands. A free country. That's okay, he can cope with that. He remembers he's left the a/c on in his office. The a/c was running on money, she isn't going to go to college and everything is all right because she thinks it's a free country. It is so absurd he wants to wave it all away with a backwards flip of his hand, and Kate, just then, leans forward so that his fingers knick her face.

"Sorry," he says.

She stares at him and puts her hand up under her nose. "What did you do?" she asks.

"Nothing," he says, trying to see where she's touching. "I just—"

"What did you do?" she yells. She looks at her hand as it comes from her face. He sees on it some drops of blood from his knuckles.

"You hit me! You hit me! You've given me a bloody nose!"

"No, Kate. No, no, it's my own blood. Look."

She doesn't look at his knuckles, she pounds the counter, crying. "You hit me! You hit everything! I hate you! No wonder no one can stand you these days. Mom can't. I hate you!"

He goes to touch her shoulder but she ducks under the counter. "You're horrible!" she shouts and runs out the door.

On the counter, a droplet of his blood is streaked like a red hair. What does she mean about Mary Ann not standing him? He can hear Kate's bike lock drop into the basket. It's an accident. He hasn't hit her. He hears the crunch of Kate cycling off and then the quiet drops like cloth.

An hour later, when Mary Ann's car pulls in, Raeburn is out stacking anchors. He's turned on the back speaker to hear the bell when customers come in. The bell hasn't rung. The thermometer says 108 but it catches the sun. It's in the upper 90s, but the humidity is high. Not a breeze, only the occasional shift of air like the movement of wet laundry.

He is stacking four anchor boxes onto the dolly, walking it to the platform edge and stacking the boxes up on it. Over and over. The weather will be like this, probably warmer, for three months. At the end of which he has to come up with twelve thousand six hundred. He thinks of an expression: today is the beginning of the rest of your indebted life. His hands go into fists, one on another, as if grabbing a vanished baseball bat.

The worst, as the blue and orange pile grows smaller on the

ground and bigger on the platform, is the sudden understanding that he's always been indebted. He is no more than Roy Higgs' uppity sharecropper, a Carl Purvis with teeth. He is stripped to his waist and keeps humping bad anchors, pouring sweat, attempting to name the worst exactly. And as Mary Ann drives up, he has it: he hates how for twenty-five years, from when he was sixteen to this morning, he's fooled himself into believing he was anything *other* than one of Higgs' holdings.

Mary Ann gets out of the car and calls up, "What happened, Bill?"

Raeburn takes out his wet handkerchief and wipes his wet face. He is shiny to his jeans. Age hasn't thickened him. His muscles are fine honed not so much from particular exercise but because each of his movements is charged; he keeps in shape by the effort of suppressing some tremendous energy, as if his life were an engagement in existential isometrics.

He looks down from the platform at his wife standing before the car with her hands on her hips. Is she accusing him? He squats. "What happened is because I wasn't here and you weren't here or at home, these anchors dropped on us again. More, this time. Remember these, the ones made for Hudson's Bay that we sent back late April?"

Out behind Mary Ann, he sees the dock stumps for their abandoned marina poking from the milky water like bad teeth.

Mary Ann says, "Home? You know I was at Marco Island doing the phone-order promotion for the store. Not the anchors. It's Kate. Why did you hit her? She's sick over it."

Raeburn stands, breathes deep and taps an anchor box with his toe. Then he kicks it. His toe hurts. "I did not hit her." He carefully moves his toes to the edge of the loading platform, as in a diving competition. "I was making a sort of dismissive movement, like this, and she happened to lean across the counter, and my hand, my fingers, grazed her. And the blood was from my hand, here. I skinned it on something this morning."

"Bill, for heaven's sake, she's lying on her bed with a bloody nose."

He jumps down to get closer, and the momentum rushes him towards her. Mary Ann jumps back from him.

"No, I wasn't going to… Did you think…? Look, I didn't hit Kate, I wasn't going to hit you. I just jumped down. Kate didn't have a bloody nose when she left."

She says, "I might have expected this, what with you going around putting your fists through the walls for years. Okay, so what happened at the bank?"

He sees his wife's earnestness as wrongheaded now, her large eyes and square shoulders carrying through, regardless. "I wouldn't hit Kate for anything, not the bank, not anything else. What has gotten into the two of you? Is it that group?"

"The Marcos Island Power Squadron? Oh, you mean our anti-oil exploration group. Kate said you were steamed up about it."

"I didn't hit her because… I mean, I didn't hit her. I wasn't steamed up. Or, I was, but… I asked her, look…" He cannot speak in the face of such accusation. It's too—the word Kate always uses—too gross. The platform edge gleams where backing trucks have scraped the steel.

She says, "Tell me about the bank."

He nods, looking at the scuffed toe of his dock shoe. "The bank. Charlie Styles read me the riot act, I mean in the polite way he says everything. But this time he added that he can't let the debt interest go because it's not going to have its usual guarantor. So I come back and first thing call Higgs." This, he knows is not true. This was third thing, after the session in the Red Parrot and the discovery of the anchor mountain.

"So what did he say?"

48

Raeburn turns and leans back against the car. "He said he couldn't go on carrying me."

"Why, I mean, why now?"

"Why now?" His question sounds like a ricochet. The roofline of the car burns against his bare shoulders. "Because we owe the bank, owe Roy, really, three hundred and thirty-six thousand, six hundred and forty-two dollars. More by now. And that doesn't count the two mortgages we got on his say-so. And I guess he said it now because he has to stop the nonsense some time."

"But why now?"

He understands her repeating the question to be merely shock; still, its stupidity goads him. "Because now he woke up to the fact that he's a businessman, not the United Way. Not the William Raeburn Disaster Relief Fund. So, end of this quarter, we pay in twelve thousand, six hundred dollars."

"But, my god, Bill, from where?"

She stands with her wide forehead frowned to a moderate chop that before this morning he would kiss smooth. This morning is another lifetime ago. "Where?" he says.

"We are not touching Kate's college fund."

"Well, we are also not touching Turtle Key Marine profits, because there aren't any. And we are not touching the house mortgage because we are mortgaged up to the hilt. So, since the business needs the pickup, we're touching my boat and your car which could total ten or ten and a half which would still leave us two short, and maybe putting in ordinary business cash would give another thousand, and the rest we'll, I don't know. Couple of my baseball trophies are silver, one's gold plate. Worth a few hundred. Garage sales? Bake sales?" The backs of his shoulders are burning from the car.

"We are not touching Kate's college fund. We have told her she wouldn't have to work, not her first year, anyhow. We've promised that."

He says, "Could you tell me something about you and this SPOIL group?"

"What is there to tell that you don't know? I do it because I don't want the Gulf choked dead with spills. Those Coastal Oil pipelines off Fort Meyers are disasters waiting for a chance."

"Here's what I know, Mary Ann. Our business is in hock, our house is in hock, and Roy Higgs just stopped handing us out food stamps. And, yes, Kate's college education. That's another real problem I know. Not dream problems like the oil spill which has not happened."

"What are you saying? The oil drilling is a real problem."

His shoulders are burning. He keeps them against the car. "No, Roy Higgs Jr. is the problem. Call that two. He is also the area's chief lobbyist for Coastal Oil, trying to bring exploration drilling down here. Call that another two. Two and two. That's not a dream, that makes four."

"Just say what you mean."

Sweat runs into his eyes. "I mean, for all I know, that's *why now*, finding out you and Kate were in that group could be what woke Roy from his sleep of reason, his dream of charity."

"Bill, that's just crazy."

Raeburn's skin has sucked all the burning from the steel. He shifts along to another hot spot. "Well, what do you think has kept us going, the wild success of TK Marine?"

"You know we were doing fine until Roy and the bank convinced us to expand in eight-six when interest was high. And then we got hit in the neck with the recession, like lots of people here. And your wonderful benefactor didn't bother to tell us he was even then set to develop the town marina which killed ours." She folds her arms.

He turns from her and looks at the shimmer off the car roof. He brings his outstretched arms down until, an inch off, he feels the heat griddle the soft skin up near his armpits. Because he's turned away, he speaks louder. "To make it clear: I know Roy's oil money is as big for him as the construction and development business. And his oil investments relate to his lobbying. He bankrolls us and one day finds that you're working against oil. Is he supposed to say and do nothing?" Raeburn's outstretched hands hover just over the car.

He senses her move up behind him. She says, "Maybe not. At least, all this time, we haven't jumped at Roy's command."

He shuts his eyes against the glare off the car roof. "Because he hasn't commanded, until now." His arms out in front of him made him think of sliding into base. "Roy brought it up in our phone call. He made it very clear: he wants the two of you out of the group. Well, I don't think he really cares about Kate, who's just a kid. You, he wants you to drop out of the group. It could help us, I mean, help Kate. So you should drop out."

He can't believe he's saying this. He brings the thick of his palms down onto the car roof. It's as if he's had these words rehearsed, as if he'd always been waiting for some sort of rotten command from Roy to which he'd been readying his agreement.

"Bill?"

He opens his eyes but can't turn to see her. His palms itch with the burning.

She says, "We can make it if, like you say, we sell the car and the boat and put in some business cash and save money at home. We could fix up the space over the back of the store and rent it as an apartment. But not Kate's college fund and no, I can't drop out of the group. What's the sense of a marine supply store if the boating stops because the water's ruined? Look what happened a few years ago across on the Texas coast."

She is thinking only of the first payment. He is seeing twelve thousand six hundred dollars payment after payment stretching from here to Texas. She doesn't get it, she has no idea of the scale of their ruin. Raeburn believes that as long as the bottoms of his arms don't actually make contact, he can stand the heat.

"Bill, you've never let Roy do this, make us afraid for ourselves."

He lets his arms come flat down onto the car roof. There is a certain relief in this worst pain. He supposes he thinks oil exploration a good thing, if it's way out, like at Fort Meyers, eighty miles offshore. The steel is impossibly hot. He doesn't move his arms.

Her voice moves to his side. "We're just his debtors, not his toadies."

His toady arms are on fire to the bone. He slowly lifts them off the car and turns. Her worried, serious, pretty face, her shaming pity, which is pitiless. He folds his arms and lightly rubs the skin.

"Mary Ann," he says, "please leave that group. I'm asking you this as my business partner. For Kate's sake. Kate doesn't have to leave the group. We just can't do everything we want."

"That's true, but the most important things, well, we have to do them. No, I won't quit the group. The hell I'll quit."

He hits her. Like that, his burnt right arm unfolding backwards, cuffing her backhanded, the same skinned knuckles as with Kate, but no accident. She spins open-mouthed along the fender. He cannot believe he's done this.

And then she comes back at him and he prepares to ward off her fists. His left forearm crosses before him as she jumps. She kicks into his groin, he goes to his knees, curling around the pain.

She is saying, "Don't you ever dare," saying it again as he struggles up, his hand cupped to his crotch. "Don't you dare. Ever, don't you ever dare."

So that she is still saying, "Ever dare, don't you ever," when he is able to take a breath enough to stand and hears a crack as of a broken bat which is him hitting her with his fist, feeling even in the instant of first contact the miserable softness of her cheek over her jawbone.

She bends back nearly double before her knees give way and she buckles sideways and falls face down into the marl.

He moves instinctively to help her, to beg, but the pain is too much and he drops on his side and pulls his knees in to catch his breath over the searing in his testicles. He hears her moan but cannot look. His underarm against his jeans is a line of boiling blisters. He thinks she may be crawling away.

Later he hears her groan and the car door opens and shuts. He thinks if there is any heart in the world she will run him over now, and then back up over him and run over him again to make sure. He hears the car drive away.

Later, the bell rings. A customer. Sorry, he thinks, the proprietor is busy out back clutching his balls after beating his wife. Please take what you want, rob the place blind, and have a nice day. He knows he will have no such luck. The customer will leave a dollar and fifty cents on the counter with a note that he's taken two lead sinkers.

Raeburn knows he's just smashed his life apart. The second time. When he slowly makes it to his feet, he sees nothing but stacks of the wrong anchors.

Chapter Three _____

T HE NIGHT I FOUND OUT about Bill and Mary Ann was long and jumpy. I'd been steadily sipping whiskey through the sets to ease what wasn't so much a craving—that had been shocked and shrunk and habituated out at the clinic—as a rush of nostalgia for the logic of cocaine, what someone in New York had called the overdrive of Mr. C Major.

Frank Edrich and I were the last two at the club, he behind the bar, doing the money with his hand-held computer, me in front of it holding an absolutely-the-last-one, two after one for the road. Frank looked up, between calculations. "Trio sounded great."

It hadn't, but I didn't contradict. Probably Ben Niles, my drummer, and I were the only ones to know better. Tony Varez, my bass, had been showing off, and I hadn't said anything about it, as a group leader should have, because I thought maybe this was Tony's way of warning me he wasn't happy about my seeing his cousin Charlene, me being the white third of the trio. Whatever, he'd ruined the trio's balance, especially on ballads. All Tony's solos had been streams of blinding, explosive chords. But what in hell was there to hear in an explosion?

I wasn't feeling very happy with myself for backing away from calling Tony on this, and I was thinking about Ginny's challenge about my presence in Turtle Key. What I actually thought, sipping the last of the drink, was that I'd once played a long gig with the great Davy Wells, and now I was playing turtle. I said goodnight to Frank, feeling very sorry for myself. When I hit the fresh air, my knees started to go on me, and I knew the Caddy would stay parked by the club as I wobbled home. Then I saw the cop car and walked over. It was Al Jarowski who for twenty bucks waited to follow Frank to First Southern's night deposit drawer. My watch said ten to three in the moonlight. Al smiled up and said, "Night, Mister B. Take it easy, now."

I tried walking a straight line from his car to the dock edge. I was frazzled, paranoid. Why had Al called me Mister B? Did he really mean Mister C for cocaine? And why Mister anything? We'd been at high school together, Christ's sake. I stood at the edge and looked at the moon. What if I called Al Mister Jerk, moonlighting in the moonlight, au clair de la lunatic? And what about that come on from Anita? The moon wasn't blue to see me without a love of my own. My love was my comfortable life. "Perdido" was a good song, too. I stood looking up. I heard Frank get into his car and drive off, and then Al's car drive off after him. At my feet was a pile of oyster shells. I put my hands into them. Lost pearls, hard shells, hard mothers, mothers of pearl. I took a handful and tried to skim them, though knew, even drunk, that they were too light and the water too far below. One, two, three, four, throwing sidearm. I saw a pearly flapping out of sight and then I heard them banging off the boats below. From down below me, someone called my name. I jumped back. Again.

"Mickey, it's Bill. Is Al still up there?"

I answered, "Wait," to the metronomes of masts. I turned to

see Frank's car pull out of the lot, followed by Al's cop car. Bill's head appeared just below the toes of my loafers. He said he needed to talk to me, out on the boat. I was too drunk to wonder about the hush-hush, but it seemed pleasant enough, since I had no other fixed engagements, Charlene either asleep at my place by now or not there. I squatted and jumped down, but my heel caught on the gunwale and I flew across the bow straight into the sea. But I hung in mid-air, my face six inches over the water. Then I was pulled back and up and in, not a drop of water on me, held as if I were a little kid. Bill had simply grabbed the back of my shirt in one hand.

"Reeled in like a little yellowtail."

Bill said nothing. He steadied me onto my feet and sat me in the fishing chair and strapped me into the safety harness. Like I was a small child, a small, drunk child. "Bigger, than a yellowtail," I said, "a Jewfish." Then we were moving past the outer moorings into the dark gulf. I tried to watch the channel markers coming up luminous reds and greens. It got me dizzy, so I listened to the quiet plashing, a nice and balanced sound, no manic bass player to spoil it. Bill was saying something about anchors.

"What anchors?"

"You haven't been listening."

I unharnessed myself to listen and lurched up to Bill at the console and fell back on the bench. Bill shoved water at me. I drank some. Bill said something about me drinking almost half a gallon of water. He was right. I signaled him to slow down and went to the gunwale to pee. "A beautiful night," I said. "Stars."

"They're all in your head. It's heavy cloud; a big tropical storm system's coming."

I sat on the bench. "I feel better," I said. But the moment I said it, sobering, I felt worse.

"We'll head out towards Loggerhead Key. Tell me when you feel up to listening."

I nodded and kept my head down to nap. Maybe Bill had run into drug runners at sea, like he had three years ago. I wondered if he still kept a gun in the boat, as he had after that. The boat was flying, forty knots, but the wind felt warm. The night was a giant hair dryer turned to HI. I was saying, "Hi, Hi." I nudged Bill to slow down and stood and went sick over the side. I wished the fish the good of all that slightly used single malt. I sat down and off we went from blowing LO back to HI.

I woke into the thick velvet of the water night. The boat was still. The air was heavy as water; it whined with gnats and mosquitoes. I heard a steady break of water and then Bill swam up and pulled himself into the boat. I found more water to drink. Bill toweled off and got into his jeans. Finally, I remembered and said, "Okay, I can listen now." He sat beside me and looked out over the wheel.

He began by telling me he'd hit Mary Ann so hard he'd broken her jaw. I must have found this so shocking that I didn't really take it in. Then he went back and told me about his debts, Old Roy, and Roy, which I pretty much knew, and then the bank meeting and the anchors and his call with Roy, and the business with Kate. And then I understood what he'd said at the beginning, so that when he went on about his argument with Mary Ann and his arms on the car roof and slapping her, I knew how it would end in his hitting her, and it shocked me even more. So when he turned his forearms up to show me the lines of blisters, I wasn't exactly moved to sympathy, and when he told me of Mary Ann kicking his balls, I smiled to myself, though I knew the bad part was coming, and I had to keep swallowing down the sickness coming to my throat. And then he told me about hitting her: he said it was the worst thing he'd done in his life. Worse than beating up his father so that his father tried to kill himself. He said Kate had called him from the hospital; it was a hairline crack in her jawbone and a broken molar, but the punch might as easily have killed her. Then he

said "Jesus," down to the floor of the boat, and I found I was saying it, too, repeating Jesus, Jesus, more to keep hearing the shriek
of the "eee," Jeeesus, who, I could imagine Ginny saying, wasn't
any god of mine. I stood up and threw a hard punch at Bill's head,
which he seemed to deflect with a shrug onto his shoulder, so I
threw another and he raised his arm and waved it away. I slumped
back onto the bench. After some time, Bill said, "I know."

"You know shit," I said, and felt so bad for Mary Ann and Bill
and Kate and myself that I got up and threw all my weight behind
a right, which Bill disappeared from, the punch pulling me past
him and over the side into the Gulf. No hand to catch me. I came
up spitting. The sea felt stupid, warm as the air and greasy. I swam
from the boat with a headache, Bill calling, "Mickey, don't be stupid." I was stupid, so I wasn't going to answer to that. I felt I was
swimming in chicken soup. Chicken, yellow, I couldn't even land
a punch, even a sneak attack punch. I was stupidly crying, as if to
salt the already over-salted soup sea. Seaweed bobbed by like matzo balls. The boat went puhtz-puhtz beside me.

"Don't be stupid. Get in."

After a while, feeling I was trading one stupidity for another, I
got back into the boat. I sat in the fishing chair and Bill roared off
full throttle. Black sky, black Gulf. I wasn't going to say another
word to Bill if we went all the way to the Yucatan. I tried to understand the moral implications of my position and fell asleep. I woke
aching and sweaty in the chair. The boat was anchored. Close
ahead was the semicircling arms of Loggerhead Key. I went forward and stood at the console with Bill. Everyone loved Loggerhead, our little atoll treasure. Tears moved down Bill's face. I
knew he was the villain, here, but I felt sorry for him. I said, "I
guess you'd better talk to me."

He started telling me how much Mary Ann had loved him.
About how shy she was when they first met. A real high school vir-
gin, and even after they first were married, how sex was for the

dark. He went on, though I wasn't comfortable with listening. How she more and more loved making love with him, how uninhibited she became. He told me some uninhibited details, words she used. I didn't want to hear but listened, fascinated. Then, after he said, "Can you imagine, she had me call her that, and loved me so much, and I just hit her like that," I hit him hard in the mouth. From out of nowhere, I suppose, from out of somewhere like where he hit Mary Ann. Bill just stood rubbing his mouth, spitting. And rather than feel any relief, I realized I'd hurt my right hand. This is the reason why most pianists don't box. He didn't give me a dirty look. I was still drunk, but I knew he was not going to treat me like he would a real man. Or a woman, come to that. I said the worst thing I could think of: "You're really your old father's son, aren't you."

"Yes."

"I mean, before his accident."

"I know."

"Really a redneck bastard." I didn't know why I said that, at the time. Now I suppose what Bill had done brought a bad memory to mind: as a kid, the day before Bill's famous playoff game, I'd seen him defend his mother by beating his father off her, when I'd been cycling out on the mangrove flats. I'd sensed he was doing the right thing, but I couldn't stick watching it.

Now here I was, a redneck bastard, I knew, going on like that. I looked at him, shoulders slumped, crying in silence, and the image I'd held, somehow, since childhood went down. Golden Bill and talented Mickey, a wife beater and dilettante drunk out in the black of the Gulf. I looked at the water. Sharks were supposed to feed off here in the deep.

I jumped in. The joke, not a good one, was on me: I stood in a foot and a half of water. My right hand hurt and I had a headache. You could, if you put your mind to it, drown in a teacup. "Get back in, will you?" Bill was crying or laughing. I was going to walk to deep water. Each step, my foot sunk in mud to my ankles. I felt close to Bill out there; that is, I felt I was feeling something like he was feeling by staying out of the boat, by this act of stupidity. The engines started. I saw they were feathered up high.

"You're walking in a shallows two miles wide."

I thought Bill might be lying to keep me from killing myself. But I knew I wasn't really going to, or else I would have fallen face first into the water and snorted mud to death. I should have been more concerned with Bill, but something of his magic, that aura I, at any rate, believed in, still kept me from thinking he was seriously in trouble. What I did was try to find a dignified gait. The *Mary Ann*—the boat was named for her—tut-tutted along side. One of my loafers came off in the mud. I was not going to stoop for it.

"Hey, I've been kicked out of my house, and I deserve it. You socked me in the mouth and I deserve it; I shouldn't have told you that personal stuff. Anyway, why the hell are *you* getting so worked up? Get back in the boat."

He was a nice guy, I thought, but for the punch. He was now very lost. I, too, was a pretty nice guy, but for several things, and also lost. Maybe I was so worked up because I'd idealised his marriage, like I had his character. Maybe I'd felt his was my own vicarious marriage. I felt sorry for both of us. "I'm sorry I hit you on the mouth."

"I deserved it," he said.

"No," I said, getting back into the boat, "because I hurt my hand."

Then Bill was maneuvering the boat across the shallows. It took a delicacy of touch nothing like a punch to his wife's face. Everything was spoiled. To the east, a line of electric blue showed over the black. False dawn. The boat came to deeper water and picked up speed.

He leaned to me and said, "I was wrong to give up baseball.

That business with my father and his hovering between life and death and then going strange, him going nuts, it was that. It got so I couldn't play ball without going through all that."

I said, "You were wrong giving up baseball and wrong not doing anything with that art history degree you got at Miami." I felt I was being reasonable without consoling him. Bill the slugger. I watched the coming on of the dark red flare line in the sky. Other than Turtle Key, a flicker of light points twenty miles away, it was impossible to separate the mainland from the mangrove islands, or the islands from the sea. I had always liked this local breakdown of boundaries (I thought of my rooftop riff for Ginny), but now it seemed just a pathetic attraction to hiding places.

Then he drove. The first sunlight reddened the boat, turning him into a slumped, terra-cotta statue of the Wounded Warrior. I felt sorry for him and thought I'd offer to help with his interest payment. It wasn't as if I was saving my money to send my kids to college. Then I thought of Bessie Smith singing about getting beat up by her man: "Ain't nobody's business if he do." But in life, Bessie had beaten any man who dared lift a finger to her, while Mary Ann had taken twenty year's of Bill's frustrations on her jaw.

Bill said, "Here's sunrise."

I looked into the cold red disc and didn't want to go home. "Can you drop me at Cal Joe's?"

"With one shoe?"

I looked. It was true. I'd left a loafer in the mud during my pointless protest. "You could wait," I said.

"No, his place gives me the creeps. All that voodoo. When I fish out that way, I avoid Cal Joe's. Anyway, I need some sleep. I can't see straight."

I remembered that Cal Joe felt the same about Bill, or, at least, was ill at ease when he was mentioned. What I felt, strange as it seemed, was that somehow Bill had hit me in the jaw, too, or had shaken something in me that I didn't want to see. So I watched the sun climb and thought of sunrise spilling over Miami Beach and crossing west to light the cocaine banks of Miami, spreading west over Calle Ocho onto garbage trucks back of Cuban restaurants, out over the suburbs to catch the grass on top of phony knolls on the too green golf courses, sunlight falling over early cars crossing the Tamiami Trail, warming the snakes that had come out of the everglades. I remembered a five-foot rattler I'd seen flattened to a snakeskin belt. I shut my eyes but the sun was flat inside them like two red pills.

The boat was winding through the mangrove islands north of town. Pale sticks marked old channels.

Bill said, "Good snapper fishing here. Sometimes I come out here and just talk."

"To who?"

"To myself. Or. When I was in college I used to have these imaginary conversations with Picasso."

"About what, socking Mary Ann?"

"Cubism. And baseball. I imagined he'd like baseball because of the old-fashioned uniforms. Or because it's like bull fighting, like a dance in which we hit a ball rather than each other."

"Oh, I see. You gave up baseball, so you have to hit Mary Ann."

"You think that's it?" Bill was asking seriously.

"No, god damn it, I don't. I don't know anything. Except it was shitty and you just better beg her to forgive you."

"Mickey, do you ever get really pissed off and sock anything? A table or a wall?"

"With the exception of you, back there, no. I take care of my fingers."

In a few minutes, the boat passed under a canopy of high mangroves and turned full into the risen sun against which Cal Joe's shack sprang suddenly on its high posts in the water. Cal Joe appeared to float up hugely beside it, his arms up in incantation.

For a second, it was as if the house was walking on its stilts straight for us.

"Damn voodoo," Bill said.

Cal Joe, short for Caloosahatchee Joe, did sometimes go in for a bit of harmless razzle dazzle, but now in the shadow of his shack I saw what I'd taken for incantation was only Joe hanging clothes out to dry on a line. He was barefoot, in red pants and a poncho shirt, with a green sash belting his big belly. I whispered, "His eyes aren't good," and called out, "Hey, Cal Joe, it's Mickey. Good morning."

Fixing a towel to the line, Cal Joe said without turning, "You never come by water before, man. And in Mr. William Raeburn's fancy boat!"

Bill called up, "How do you know it's mine if you don't see well?"

Cal Joe turned. "Don't mean I'm deaf or dumb. Know that boat sound cause you fish by here. Seen you close from in my little boat in the mangroves. Well, well. Sure is something, a visit from Jason and his Argue-not."

"Not from me, I'm just dropping Mickey off."

The boat slipped to the ladder and I pulled myself up. My arms ached and my hand hurt. The boat reversed below me.

Cal Joe went to the back rail of the deck. "William? I know I ain't seen you in years, but I'm here. Here and waitin' for you."

Bill neither answered nor looked back. He tuned the boat and it slid from the lagoon into the channel under the mangroves.

Cal Joe said, "I know he's hurtin. Bad news travels fast, a man puts his good wife in hospital." He came up to me. "Now lemme get hold them good piano hands, Mickey. Huh, my man, my main *mensch*."

In Joe's large, leather hands, my own hurt hand felt better.

"They good black hands, Mickey. Your best friends and you listen to them."

The sun was full on Cal Joe's big patchwork face, a mottle of dark browns, pale whites, red coppers. His features, too, kept shifting. Front on, his nostrils were flared West African, but his nose in profile had a long Mayan curve. In the sixties and seventies and into the eighties, Joe had farmed a little marijuana. Now he lived on social security and money from some men, black and white, for whom, like for me, he was seer or sage or clown or father confessor. To which in my particular case, was added some awareness of racism and guilt and its symptomatic patronage.

As always, when I crossed the threshold of Cal Joe's, I shut my eyes to concentrate on the smell, a mix of nutmeg, sweat, and pepper. The place was one square room with a gas cooking ring and cold water sink the landward side, the toilet being a lean-to on the seaward deck with a bucket on a line and a hole in a plank over the Gulf of Florida. The room had a blue wooden table and chair, a brown leatherette armchair and shelves of various sized wooden boxes and drawers nailed to the walls. In one corner was an iron bed too short for Joe's six-four frame.

Once I'd seen Joe asleep on it, curled into a ball of contortionist tightness. Later, Joe explained that people mostly misunderstood sleep: you had to concentrate yourself mind and body to get the most from it. Like other of Joe's maxims, it was memorable yet rationally flawed. Before his eyes had gone, Joe had read Greek mythology and decided he was like old Proteus.

This morning he poured coffee from an iron pot into tin mugs and dropped in some condensed milk. I took one and sat in the armchair, and Joe took his habitual seat on the edge of the bed. The coffee was brewed with chicory and sugar, and with the condensed milk it tasted like a child's bedtime drink, vaguely medicinal and comforting. Joe fitted on a red headband with one white egret feather, as a doctor might his ophthalmoscope. "Well," he said, "what's happenin?"

Something made me say, "Bill once said you couldn't be a Caloosahatchee Indian."

"Mean how they died out five, six generations back? Yeah, your pal got the facts, but that don't mean he's right. And is that what you here for, put down this old nigger injun?"

"No, because I feel bad, not just hung over."

"Don't need me to see that."

"I think I was drinking because I got scared of wanting cocaine. But why I wanted the coke, I don't know. Anyway, so then Bill turns up in the boat and off we go out to Loggerhead Key and he tells me about hitting Mary Ann. Christ. It just got me so jumpy. Jumpier."

Cal Joe rubbed his knee. "Arthritis tellin me a storm's comin. That and the weather report on the radio." He smiled and sipped coffee. His belly between his legs moved like a green-banded beach ball.

I said, "I think I'm getting tired of this one-night-stand life of mine, Cal Joe."

"Gonna tell you somethin, maybe you know, maybe not. Mickey, you mother was one beautiful woman. No disrespect, man, but she make me weep about the color bar, make me dream of integration."

I felt strange to hear this; I hoped it wasn't because I was hearing it from a black man. Cal Joe's eyes were closed, imagining my mother. I myself couldn't; not fifteen years after she died, not a month after, come to that.

Cal Joe went on: "Most beautiful black hair. Pale skin. Celia Berman never went for suntannin, knew better. And dressed! There was a dresser, never mind your Miss Anitas. Dresses, suits, slacks, scarves—man, she had it down. And you her only child, her little man. That's a tough act for a boy, specially old Sam treat her like she was Lena Horne and the Queen of France all in one. Point is, you put your perfect mother up there, how's a real woman gonna compare? Like Celia was maybe too cool and far away for a son. Like she some statue of Afro-ditty."

Between the floorboards I saw the glitter off the water. "Are you saying I have a thing, a complex, about her?"

Cal Joe struggled up from the bed. "Goddamn, I'm getting too old to be so fat. Used to be near skinny as you." He took a pair of glasses off a shelf and put them on. Behind the lenses, his enlarged eyes looked like fish swimming in milk. "I don't much hold with that theory all us men be secret motherfuckers. What seems sense about that Eddy-pussy story is how you can haul your ass from Corinth, but you gonna meet your ass at Thebes. Dig?"

I dug: New York and Turtle Key. I stood and peeled three fifty-dollar bills from my wet wallet and put them in the coffee can over the sink. "I have to go."

"Hey, thanks. You know I'm takin the money only cause you can afford it and I make you think some and you take it more to heart when it cost, and then cause Social Security treat me like shit and pay worse, and cause it make you feel kind. Most, though, cause I really need it."

We shook hands. Cal Joe said, "Well, Jews like us got to stick together."

"So now you're Jewish, too?"

"Didn't say that. Said Jews *like us*. Hey, you not gonna walk a mile on coral in one shoe. You borrow them rubber sandals out there."

Outside, I stepped out of my loafer into Joe's sandals. The lyrics went, "Momma may have, Poppa may have, But God bless the child that's got his own." His own *what*, I wondered, as I walked the plank down to the shore.

Behind me, Cal Joe called, "And you tell Mr. William Raeburn he gonna have to see me soon."

II. Tropical Depression

Chapter Four _____

I'D NEVER MUCH LIKED ROY. No real reason, I just accepted the conventional wisdom that despite his great business success he wasn't a good old boy like his father, Old Roy. In our few social meetings as adults, I'd developed a slight disdain; behind his elegant, custom-made clothes, I saw Roy as if on the verge of sweat and dishevelment, from the strain of climbing to the class he'd married. In my attitude was certainly something of my Jewish outsider's view; more comfortable was my musician's view that Roy just wasn't cool or hip.

Bill, on the other hand, had real reasons for disliking Roy. Roy had driven Bill into serious debt by providing financing for a marina project he himself made worthless when he developed a better-located marina. Turtle Key wisdom put this down to the carelessness of the very rich, but I suspected there was jealousy at work: Roy had to hurt Bill because he felt his father had loved Bill more than him.

So it was something of a surprise when the Friday after my

night at sea with Bill, Roy called to invite me to go up to Cape Buena with him the next day for the opening of the turtle museum and sanctuary he'd endowed. Just the two of us; he said Anita couldn't make it and he thought it would be fun to go up with "an old TK buddy." I glanced around my living room but saw no one else. Then I said sure, it would be fun. I was actually curious to see if Roy would say anything about his fight with Anita. Besides, Charlene was in Atlanta on a job interview and I wanted some company. I knew I should have made more of an effort to see Bill, who was living alone over his store, confused and miserable, but I felt uncomfortable with the weight of his rambling confessions. Anyhow, I told myself Bill was buried in work.

At ten the next morning, I stood outside the building looking for Roy's sedate old model station wagon, not "estate," the kind of car Anita's old money taught him to drive. A hot, light rain was beginning to fall when a new red Porsche convertible pulled up and beeped. Roy was at the wheel. I got in. He told me I looked sharp. I put my jacket in back, over his. "Speaking of sharp," I said, "is this your car?"

"Yes. Picked it up three days ago. I was... You know, sometimes you have to get... Spoil yourself a little, sometimes. Know what I mean?"

I said, "I've made it a life study." Maybe the Porsche was solace for his fight with Anita. I strapped myself in and we drove off. Too fast—the wheels spun and the back tire banged into the curb. "Wet," I said.

Roy said, "One hell of a machine," and concentrated on gears, clutch, brakes and accelerator. He was an awful driver, and the weather didn't help. By the time we got to the coast road out of town, a tropical depression was on us. The wind had picked up so that the fronds on the roadside coconut palms rose and flipped and suddenly flopped over like wet mops. Sheet rain came billowing through straight-down rain that whacked on the windshield in clots the size of fists. Usually, I like wild weather, but not with someone having to work so hard to keep a Porsche on the road at thirty.

I said, "Hope this doesn't ruin the opening."

"Hell," he said, "there'll be lots of food and drink: tornadoes wouldn't keep this crowd away, all the state and county freeloaders, not to mention the press, maybe some TV."

I went back to trying to ignore the driving and enjoy the storm. After a while, Roy said, "You're pretty tight with Bill Raeburn."

"I suppose."

"Guess about everyone's heard about him socking Mary Ann, getting kicked out of his own house."

"Yeah, it's a mess."

"Just like that, wham, bam, thank you, ma'm. And cracked her jaw."

"Well, I don't think it was 'just like that.' Bill was at his wits' end. Big financial problems, but, of course, you'd know more about them, Roy."

"Oh, you're not going to give me a hard time now, are you?"

The windscreens pushed back waves of rain. Water came over the blades. "No," I said, "I'm not someone who gives anyone a hard time."

We drove in the steady hiss of tires and dull roar of hard rain on the soft roof. We hadn't spoken for about half an hour when Roy said, "Nevertheless, can't help thinking about it. Wife keeps getting at you, getting at you, getting at you. And then—boom! Yessir, that argument is absolutely over." He glanced at me with a slight smile.

"No," I said, "it's not over. Except in the sense that Mary Ann's left him, pretty much, because of it. Is that what you mean?"

"No, no. It's terrible, I know that. I'd never do anything like

71

that to Anita. And not just because she can probably beat the shit out of me in a serious fight."

I tried to imagine Anita doing that. It wasn't difficult. The wipers kept sweeping away the water, which kept climbing right back. Thump, thump, thump.

"Mickey, maybe you can't know what I'm talking about. You've never been married. You ever lived with a woman for any real time?"

"With one woman for three years, then with another woman for four. But you're right: I've never thought of doing that."

"Now old Bill, you ask me, he should have stuck to playing baseball. There's the crux of it. You have a talent that big, like him, that and a love for the game, you have to go with it or it'll warp your life if you don't."

"You could be right about that. On the other hand, lots of other things can come up—emotionally, temperamentally, economically."

Roy said, "Bullshit." Then he said, "Hell, I didn't mean like you and piano playing. Besides, you still do that."

I said, "I know you didn't. So do you have a speech written out for this event, or notes?"

"Never. But I have it all down." He tapped the side of his head and quickly brought his hand back to the wheel.

When we turned off Route 41 onto the dented two-lane to Cape Buena, Roy got excited and put the Porsche down to first and then, too fast, into second, so that the engine ground down and went flat at about zero rpms. He pulled over and stopped. "Guess I am thinking about the museum thing. Do me a favor and drive?"

I couldn't do it worse than Roy. We got out, got our shirts soaked and switched seats. It was a beautiful machine. I'd driven older models. I had about ten minutes of fun when we ran into the end of the traffic jam headed for the museum, the only building on the Cape. "Pull out and drive down the other lane. Hell, I'm the guest of honor, right?"

I shrugged, put on the high beams and pulled out with the safety lights flashing. Not my driving style. After a mile, we were stopped by a policeman in a slicker. Roy stuck his head out, introduced himself, complimented the cop on the great traffic control job, and we were waved on. When we came into the circular drive in front of the museum, we were surrounded by legs and umbrellas. We put on our jackets and I found myself shaking hands after Roy shook them. The first was Tom McColl's. He was the jolly, roly-poly museum and sanctuary director. He said to Roy, "You've never seen the finished place, have you?" Roy said, "No," and, keeping his head down under the umbrella, continued: "It's just great, wonderful, Tom. It's terrific."

I was looking at a building in contemporary Florida Rustic— plate glass with log-like trim. It suggested a Seminole lodge, or a fishing camp, or whatever green nostalgic mush you were into. Cameras were flashing like lightning in the rain. Someone held a mike out over a video camera.

The crowd on the front deck followed us into the foyer. McColl told Roy that everyone was so grateful to him for this. Roy modestly said no, it was nothing at all. He turned and whispered to me: "He thinks I'm kidding: mostly I got some Coastal Oil Foundation money shoved this way."

The crowd closed around us. McColl apologized for the weather forcing all the ceremonies inside. Then he apologized for the a/c going down. Roy said, "Never apologize and never mind, Tom. I like the smell of a friendly crowd." A waiter squeezed in with a tray of bourbon on the rocks. The foyer walls were encircled with pretty turtle photos: turtles underwater and on beaches, hatching from eggs and going back into the sea. A state senator came up with an entourage of at least twenty people. Then four county commissioners squeezed in. Then everyone made room for some reporters, one CNN type who could afford to be very low key as Roy and McColl and all the other localish bigwigs were practically bowing to him with civility, a reporter from Fort Myers and, lo and behold, Dee Dee Prentice, whom I'd dated a few years before, who worked out of Naples and doubled for the Turtle Key Globe. When we kissed cheeks, Roy pulled himself away from the bigger fry to say, "Great. Friends in the press. How you all doing?" Roy was on his second bourbon.

We squeezed into the main display room where Roy and Mc-Coll posed for photographs and gave statements. I got lost in a corner and watched. McColl introduced Roy to the patrons. They wore red ribbons with gold lettering saying SPOTS, which, I was told, was Special Pals of Turtles. Roy was phenomenal: courtly with the ladies and jokey with the gents. A lot of laughter. McColl kept wiping his face with Kleenex. He moved Roy around the luncheon tables to the exhibits with a series of "Scuse us" and some respectable downfield blocks. I moved around to see what they were looking at. It was a series of photos of the old turtle canning industry at Turtle Key. Roy was telling McColl how Old Roy used to show him the wrecked buildings out on the docks. McColl was beaming. His fat hand flipped out to narrate the blown-up photos. Long wooden sheds and holding kraals that I remembered derelict from my childhood. Then came photos of the old wooden schooners, black crews shiny with sweat posed stiffly by turtles hanging from deck cranes. More blurred, a photo of men bent gaffing turtles aboard and over the deck. All sorts of turtles—hawksbills and loggerheads and leatherbacks. McColl was pointing to a picture of overturned turtles, helpless as soup plates.

I came up closer. Roy was sipping another drink, his smile gone. McColl was already on to narrating the next display, where photos were flanked by four-foot poles onto which were attached two-foot steel blades. The photos between them showed men using these same big knives, slicing out the live flesh, and stirring the full boiling kettles; and in the last photo, stacks of empty turtle shells.

Roy stopped McColl in full flow and pulled close to him: "God, Tom, I thought I was funding a sanctuary here, not some damn turtle holocaust museum."

"But, Roy, it's what endangered them. Roy, we kept sending you all the details of the displays and you didn't object."

"How in hell am I supposed to look at every last thing?"

McColl was continually wiping his face, grinning on the verge of tears: "Anyhow, it's the sanctuary part outside, the sheds and pens and clinic that make the place upbeat."

Roy set his empty on a tray and took another bourbon. "Okay, sure, sure. Don't worry, Tom. Just a bit of a shock. Really effective." He threw an arm around McColl's shoulders. "Look, it's terrific. A terrific place and we'll open it in style."

Though it was McColl who kept mopping the sweat off his face, it was Roy who seemed to me more affected by the heat and crowd and airlessness as he smiled and laughed and looked interested and was terribly nice to everyone. The drink he was knocking back couldn't have helped. His skin had gone the red of a crawfish in a bloody Mary. Maybe he was out of his natural element, which I guessed consisted of meetings in the land acquisition and planning stages of the thousand unit housing tracts and square mile shopping malls with which he was covering southwest Florida.

At one point, as we inched around the packed room, he waited for me to catch up and whispered, "Shit, as a kid, I used to love the little cubes of turtle in the soup. Made Old Roy laugh when I called it 'fish Jell-O.'"

Then we were out in the foyer again. Some spots cleared a space before a curtained wall plaque. McColl took a mike and thanked everyone for coming out in lousy weather that "anyhow is good for turtles." Then he launched into a long praise of Roy. Roy listened with his eyes on his shoes, enjoying himself. In the applause, he hugged McColl like a lost brother. Then he took the mike.

He thanked McColl, he thanked the SPOTS, he thanked the State and County politicians and he thought all of them should thank their lucky stars the place had such a great director. McColl out-beamed himself. Then Roy frowned and stood silent. As a musician, I dug his timing. He began to speak, quietly, of the bad old days for turtles, so movingly displayed in the next room. His voice dropped to a more somber register: he spoke of an industry that took and took without a thought of giving back. He stopped. He lifted his head and began to smile. I dug his rhythm. He turned to McColl and said Tom had over praised him something shameful—not that he'd minded—because (he waited for the laughs to stop) because he was only a link. He named two or three people who'd handled the details, done, he said, the hard work. But (now speaking through the light applause) the real praise had to go to the folks at Coastal Oil who'd shown again and again that an enlightened partnership between business and natural resource management could change the world for good. I remember thinking "for good" could mean "forever," but I don't think others heard it like that. Roy said, hell, he was just honored he'd been able to make this contribution to the ongoing partnership between industry and the wonderful local environment. And he was proud to officially declare open the Roy Higgs Junior–Coastal Oil Collins County Florida Turtle Sanctuary and Museum.

The man, I had to give him that, had the true populist tone and phrasing. He pulled the curtain cord but nothing happened. He pulled harder. It was stuck. He yanked it and the cord broke off, so he pulled back the shiny blue curtains with his hands and for a moment stood blocking it from view. Then he stepped aside in the applause with a strange smile, as if slightly shocked by seeing the very words he'd last spoken instantly turned to bronze before his eyes.

McColl announced lunch. Someone called, "Questions?" It was Dee Dee. McColl was saying "No," but Roy took back the mike. "It's okay, Tom. Just a few." He nodded over the crowd.

"Thanks. Dee Dee Prentice, Confederated Gulf Newspapers. In light of your being one of the South's biggest oil lobbyists, how would you answer local critics who maintain that Coastal's plans for offshore drilling aren't 'enlightened,' to use your phrase—that they endanger not only turtles but the entire lower Gulf eco-system?"

McColl looked like he wished Dee Dee was a turtle, one of those in the messy photos. But Roy was smiling. "Well, now, 'in light' of this, 'enlightened' that... Dee Dee, that's a whole lot of light, but I'm afraid I'm still in the dark. Who are all these local critics?"

"Well, SPOIL, for one."

"You don't mean they're going to spoil all these good people's lunch?"

She blushed in the laughter. "It's an anti-oil-drilling group, based in Turtle Key. SPOIL stands for Stop Pollution by the Oil Interest Lobby."

Roy was smiling kindly; he knew all the people here were on his side. "And who would these SPOIL people be when they're at home?"

Dee Dee said, "They're not at home, they're here now." She pointed back to the entrance.

I turned and saw a half dozen or so people in green rain ponchos standing down on the grass by the drive. I made out the signs COASTAL HURTS TURTLES and DRILLING—SPILLING—KILLING. A few people in the foyer began booing, but Roy said, "Hey, no. Good for them. It's a free country. Okay, here's how I'd answer them, or, more's the point, someone like Dee Dee who has the courtesy to ask: Remember how people like those out there cried that Coastal's Bonita Field here off Fort Meyers was going to be a disaster? First when they drilled, then when they put in the wells, then with the pipelines? Well, it's been producing big for four years now, and in that time the data from Loggerhead Key shows more turtles nesting and more live hatches each year. Hey, ask Tom, here. He's the expert."

McColl nodded seriously.

Dee Dee said, "Mr. Higgs, are you saying that *because* of the Bonita Field the turtles are doing better?"

"Since the field went in, Coastal has increased its very significant contributions to clearance campaigns around the Gulf, from Brownsville to Key West. So, yes, Dee Dee, you bet, in that way the Bonita Field *has* helped the turtles."

McColl led the applause, took the mike and said, "Let's eat," and ran interference for us into lunch. Roy, as we followed, said, "Hey, your friend pretty Miss Dee Dee: how's about you being very nice to her and telling her to take it easy on me."

I said, "But being very nice to Dee Dee, I couldn't tell her that. Now, if you wanted me to be real nasty... But, of course, I wouldn't do that."

He put a hand on my shoulder and looked at me as if he were seriously disappointed. As if the bad ride in his Porsche and the bourbon with melted ice I hadn't touched made me his man. Then he laughed, "Course not, Mickey. Only kidding."

During lunch, I moved away from Roy. I found Dee Dee, who asked what I was doing there. I said I was just along for the ride. Together, we added, "As always." Across from us, Roy continued shaking hands and leaning in closer to the ladies as he ate shrimp and knocked back white wine. Occasionally his voice rose over the hubbub with words like "Sure is" and "Sure do." And when a locally famous county commissioner, an iron-hard old woman, brought him another plate piled pink with shrimp, he bowed deep and kissed both her cheeks. Later, I rejoined him when I saw he was with Dee Dee. She was saying, "So, off the record, then, how would you argue Coastal's Texas oil spills helped turtles?"

Roy stepped close to her. "I wouldn't. Off the record or on, that was one damn mess. But that Brownsville Gamma Field business was ten, eleven years ago. And it couldn't happen now."

"Why not? What if this storm became a big hurricane and the Fort Meyers pipelines snapped?"

"No way, Dee Dee. First, they're state of the art strong and flexible. Second, even if they broke, which they can't, the pumps are programmed to stop pumping from depot flow valve stoppage. Third, even if the computers went wrong, which they can't, there are manual over-rides to seal off the pumps."

I moved off, not wanting to cramp Dee Dee's style nor be asked any more favors by Roy. Fifteen minutes later, I was washing my face in the men's room, tying not to listen to someone being very sick in one of the stalls. The retching stopped and Roy came out, jacket over his arm, shirt plastered to his chest. He wasn't aware of me. He went to the next basin and ran cold water over his head. By the time he pushed himself upright, I had a bunch of paper towels to hand him. He wiped his face and hands and shirt, spat in the basin and took a few deep breaths.

"Okay, I'm okay now. Bad shrimp, I think. And too much booze too fast. Damn, damn them."

"Damn who, Roy?"

"All those green fuckasses, environmental jack-offs. You know why Coastal's going to win the fight to drill off Turtle Key?"

I understood his question was rhetorical, but I answered. "Because you're going to spread enough money to bribe and otherwise influence politicians?"

"No, not that. No, it's because most of these fucks who cry about loving the sea and the Everglades are scared of any *real* nature. You look at them closely on those neat little Everglades boardwalks, and they are terrified." He wiped another paper towel over his face. "You could turn the Everglades into a parking lot and most of them could care less. Long as they had their National Geographic videos and could sit there with their potato chips watching that lioness bring down the antelope. Rerun and rerun it, munching away as that big cat tore down that antelope over and over and over."

"Let me guess, Roy: this is really off the record."

Roy leaned back against the sink. He was in bad shape, red and pot bellied and breathing hard. "Course it is. Course I didn't mean... Just kiddin, lettin off steam." Then he busied himself with his shirt and jacket and combed the blond wisps of hair that made him look balder. In the corridor, he decided we should duck out the back door for some air, rain or no rain.

Outside, the air was a little fresher, but not much. We stood under the eaves watching the rain come down from a sky of brown soup. Out in the turtle pens, something yellow moved, maybe a turtle beak breaking from the water. "Oh, yes," Roy said, "this is a lot better." I followed him around the side deck, keeping close to the building to stay dry. As we came around to the front, Roy stopped and watched the SPOIL demonstrators. "Look at them," he said, "bunch of pathetic TK losers." They did look pathetic, at most a dozen in their cheap green ponchos, walking a slow bedraggled circle. I made out the placards I'd seen before.

"Hey, look there, Mickey."

Around came a different one, held high: ROY HIGGS JR. IS OIL SCUM.

Roy said, "Not only pathetic, that is dumb as horseshit. It makes the papers and they're gonna be seen as the small-minded hysterical women they mostly are. Jesus, I could almost feel sorry for them."

I was about to give some mild reply when I made out who was

carrying the sign. Then I saw that Roy had, too. He backed onto the side deck. "You see who that is, Mickey? Oh, good goddamn. Goddamn her, all the local papers gonna have a field day. Fuckin field fuckin day, Anita paradin out there with that. My own wife and where's her Georgetown goddamned townhouse and upper East Side apartment come from but her daddy's damn oil scum money? I say local papers? My own wife protestin me like that you don't think Miami will pick it up and why not the goddamn *Washington Post* and *New York Times* and our friend inside from CNN get their cheap fuckin laughs, too? And what the hell you laughin at?"

"I'm trying not to, Roy, but, damn it, it's funny, man."

"You want to see something funny? I'll show you," he said. He went to the front deck and ran down the stairs. I went right after him: it looked to be worth getting wet for.

As Anita came around again with ROY HIGGS JR IS OIL SCUM Roy jumped in front of her and grabbed her shoulders. "Are you having fun?" he asked.

"Yes, I am," she said. "And doing something useful."

Other pickets surrounded them. I nodded at Kate and Mary Ann Raeburn whose face was still black and blue. People started coming from inside, spilling down the wide steps into the rain. Anita was startling: with her poncho blown tight to her breasts and thighs she looked pissed off and sexy. Roy held her at arms' length by her shoulders. The rain dripped off her poncho hood onto her nose, and she held up the placard as if about to bring it down on Roy's hot red skull. Suddenly, he let go her shoulders, pulled back her hood and kissed her. She shook to break free, but Roy put his arms behind her and pulled her tight to him, and the sign saying he was oil scum went down behind his back. Cameras were flashing, a sound boom swung in over them, videos whirred. What Roy was doing may have come from an instinct for stealing publicity, but it was sexual, too. I couldn't swear Anita kissed him back, but she didn't seem to struggle hard. And when Roy broke from the clinch and stepped back, there was no mistaking the rise in his trousers.

By this time, an amused pandemonium had developed around us, SPOILS and SPOTS, well-wishers and freeloaders, the press, TV, politicians. McColl pushed himself in with "Should we get these troublemakers off the property?" Roy said, "Of course not." He whispered to get his car brought round, and then he ran to the top of the stairs, pushed the rain from over his eyes and held up his hands. Even the placards went down to hear him.

"Friends," he said, "and I mean every one of y'all, protesters, too, we all want the same thing—a good life in a good environment." He looked over to where the car was coming around and then he looked my way, so I moved to the driver's side. Roy continued: "And we're also united, most united, in living some place where we can freely argue out our differences—in the great United States of America." He slowly descended the steps under McColl's high umbrella. Just before the bottom, he raised his hands again: "God bless you all, folks," he said, "and God bless America." Then he moved quickly to the Porsche and we got in and I drove with a police car leading us out.

"What did you think of that?" he asked.

I said, "I don't know: it was either the last defense of a scoundrel or you were running for president."

That seemed to cool his fire. The next thing he said, twenty minutes later, after the police car had left us and we'd come onto Route 41, was he'd have to call some favors in from TV and the press. He took out a cell phone and said, "You really think I should have seen the funny side, don't you?"

"I do, Roy."

"You and fucking Raeburn. Why is it everyone thinks you two are so cool and I'm not? Because I don't quit? Because I succeed so well?"

I wasn't going to rise to it. "It's a nice car," I said.

"Nice, I can't even drive the fucking thing. Want it? I'll give you a good deal."

"No thanks."

"Alright, Mickey, what's so funny now?"

"Nothing," I said. But I couldn't stop smiling.

Chapter Five _____

I WAS RELIEVED when Bill called to ask a favor; I could think I'd been on the verge of calling him. He wanted company on a visit to his father. Everybody knew he didn't visit Bob Raeburn. That was left to his sister Eleanor, though she, too, detested the old man. But then, she was a daughter.

I picked him up in the Caddy. The rain had stopped, temporarily, but I kept the roof up against the crazy weather. Days of downpour, days of gales and then, like this one, a day or two of such wet, gray green stillness, you felt the air was turning to slime. Bill got in, thanked me and then went quiet. We drove out to Sunset Road, locally called the Garbage Coast or, by the Cubans, *La Costa del Caca,* for its three massive hills of trash which made up the city dump. After the dump came a canal bridge and then a quarter mile of scrub until the road ran out near the water in a loop. At the top of the loop, where I turned in, was the Sunset Nursing and Retirement Home, "Collins County Caring," it said at the bottom of the sign.

Bill said, "Yeah, the county cares enough to put the place out on its cheapest land. Most of the folk here can't see well enough to see the hills of garbage, but neither can they see out their screened porches to the gulf. Just as well, as the county's cared enough to store all those dumpsters between here and the water." I didn't think he was complaining on his father's behalf. Then he asked me to come in with him, to make sure, he said, "I don't, you know, beat the old madman to death."

We walked in and along a corridor. The place seemed empty. "When was the last time you saw him?"

"Ten years ago. I know because Eleanor told me when I called to ask his room number."

"How is Eleanor?"

"She didn't say. She's very close to Mary Ann. She doesn't really want to talk to me. She did say Bob lives in a perpetual state of religious conversion—to whatever sect has got to him last."

"Things can only get better."

"You think? Well, watch this. I'm going to try asking the old man about that day before the playoff, when I beat him up."

"Why? I've told you several times over the years that I was out there bicycling. I saw you stop him beating up your mother."

"But you didn't stay. I beat him badly, Mickey. I put him into this nursing home surely as if I'd cut that towing cable myself and whipped it across Bob's head."

"Okay, so you were young and crazy. But you stopped him the only way you could, by hitting him."

"But I think something else happened out there, that I've suppressed. I get this feeling about it when I try to understand why I hit Mary Ann."

"Like what could have happened?"

"I don't know. That's why I'm here."

He opened a door. The room was small and dark with fake wood furniture. Like the rest of the place, it smelled of piss and disinfectant. Bob Raeburn sat in a rocking chair on the screened deck outside. I recalled a big, rough looking man with a broken nose and red veined cheeks, the face of a brawling drunk, my father had said. Under his short white hair, I recognized him. But there was a strangeness now, not so much of aging but as if his face were under a heavy glaze. His eyes and features looked smeared, like a Francis Bacon portrait.

Bill pulled up a chair. "Hello, Bob. Here's Mickey Berman."

Nothing, not a flicker. I nodded and sat further off.

"Bob, this is me, Bill."

The white head moved forward. He stared. "How's your mother?" His voice was hoarse and quiet.

"Mother's dead, Bob. She died twenty years ago."

His father took a pad of paper from the table beside him. "Listen to this." He held the pad sideways at arm's length and read: " 'For as much then as Christ hath suffered for us in the flesh, arm yourselves likewise with the same mind: for he that hath suffered in the flesh hath ceased from sin.' Pretty good."

"What is that?"

"Paul's First Epistle. You know, Mrs. Smith visits. She's black but she gave it to me. She's Church of God of Prophecy, which is full of wisdom. Pretty good."

Bill turned to me and tapped his head. He said, "Bob, I want to ask you about that day I hit you, the day before your accident."

"Listen to this." He held out the pad. "Hebrews, Twelve, One. '…let us lay aside every weight, and the sin which doth so easily beset us.' "

"You know what he's reading from, Mickey? He's copied out these quotes from a handout. Bob, I've done something bad. I've hit my wife. Hard. You remember that? How you hit your wife, my mother?"

Bob Raeburn said, in the same low, glazed voice, "Here's one about the wicked. It says they're 'Raging waves of the sea, foaming out their own shame.' Pretty good. Epistle of Jude."

"I came across you out in the mangroves beating up mother and I told you to stop and you wouldn't, so I pushed you off and you started coming at me and I hit you in the stomach and you sat down winded, but I didn't stop, I pulled you up and hit you in the face, beat you up pretty bad."

"Pretty good. 'For whosoever shall keep the whole law, and yet offend in one point, he is guilty of all.' That is real prophecy. Mrs. Smith, she's black, was saying this yesterday. That's Paul, not Mrs. Smith."

"Bob, what I remember is then I took mother away, took her home. Is that right?"

"Listen: 'I stood upon the sand of the sea, and saw a beast rise up out of the sea, having seven heads and ten horns, and upon his horns ten crowns, and upon his heads the name of blasphemy.' "

He hadn't read that. He had that by heart.

"Bob, if you could remember, maybe I can stop my own sickness."

His father wasn't looking at him. He said, " 'The day of the Lord will come as a thief in the night: in the which the heavens shall pass away with a great noise, and the elements shall melt with fervent heat, the earth also and the works that are therein shall be burned up.' Pretty good."

"You don't fool me, you old bastard."

I said, "Bill," and touched his shoulder.

"Sure. Let's go."

Outside, Bill stood by the car, watching an old man hunched over two canes on the grass, by the trees. The man was looking down and pushing something away, first with one trainer and then the other. But it turned out to be how he walked, an inching forward on tiny swings of each cane. Bill said, "Look at those trees next to him."

Their leaves drooped in clusters, and their trunks were cinnamon colored, splotched with black.

"Poisonwood," Bill said. "What's to keep him from tottering

and grabbing hold of a poisonwood for support? His hands would swell up and an allergic reaction shoot into his heart faster than he can walk. Goddamn this county, too mean to cut the poisonwood around its nursing home. Are we all supposed to end up like that, or like Bob?"

I suggested he get in the car. The day was looking even worse. The center of the dark sky had whitened so that it looked like a sore. As we came to the dump, Bill asked me to stop. I pulled in along the wire fence.

"Eleanor thinks I should be prosecuted for attempted murder."

"No, your sister couldn't really mean that."

"She says Mary Ann is the best thing that ever happened to her by way of marriage."

I thought of Eleanor's ex-husband and two bad kids and saw what she meant.

Bill nodded towards the dump. "Look at the turkey buzzards work that slope, taking a few big jumps and digging in. Eleanor got so mad, finally, I asked her to give me a break. Which got her madder. She said, a break? She said she left home at fourteen and warned our father she was on to him, to give me a break. And she looked after me from over our Aunt Susan's house, to give me a break. And she gave me books and talked about art and convinced me to go to U. Miami where I could meet people besides jocks or aggies, to give me a break. And when I quit baseball because it was depressing me and really hanging up my courses and they pulled my scholarship, she gave me a break by squaring it with old man Higgs. She said the trouble was she'd given me too many breaks. Everyone had, she said, because they were stuck in the past like me, and I was just another pathetic aging ex-high school hero who'd never grown up."

"That's not so. You've been responsible and worked hard for your family. You've been screwed over by Roy."

"The problem with these buzzards, close to, is that, like their eyes, their entire bald heads look bloodshot. Unreasoning, without the airborne elegance they have. Those are the eyes and heads of mean, mad drunks. Just jump and jump and dig in."

"Let's go, man. You're getting way too morbid."

"Remember when I had the pickup truck with a marlin on the passenger door and Picasso's 'Still Life with Bottle' on mine, and the town joke—maybe you started it—went, 'How'd your door get so scratched up?' "

"I remember."

"Well, now I'm the town joke. Another TK battering bastard, and not even drunk."

I started the car. "That's not so."

Bill called out the window: "Hey, buzzards, what do you know?" He said, "Look at them turn those red veined heads and jump away up the garbage and dig in. Oh, they know, Mickey, they know."

Whatever it was they knew or Bill knew, I didn't want to. I wanted to get back and play some piano before the sky dumped on us again.

One hell of a storm broke that night. The club's tin roofs roared with rain, and I kept thinking of Bill. I phoned him during the breaks, but he wasn't in or wasn't answering. After we closed up, I drove out to TK Marine, and when I saw the lights on upstairs, I pulled in and rang the back door, found it open and went up. Bill was sitting wrapped in a blanket, an empty bottle of tequila on the table beside him. He was out of his head drunk, babbling on to me about how he'd just drowned himself and had come back from the dead. Something about how he'd been saved by Joan of Arc and Picasso. I kept agreeing with him and got him to bed. He grabbed my hand and promised he wouldn't do anything foolish again, he'd figured everything out. He made me promise not to speak again about what he'd done. I told him he'd better see a doctor about the sores on his arm. I suppose I didn't really believe his suicide rant, but even if I had, I don't see that anything would have changed. The days that summer had such inevitability, by which I mean, we had.

Chapter Six _____

THE WAVES COME AT HIM STEADILY. They march through the *Mary Ann*'s spotlight and sink or slam into the hull in strict formation. At times, Raeburn can slip the boat across two or three, pitch up, and run several more into another cycle. He knows that because the waves are calculus and the boat only crude approximation, he more often rolls into twelve to fifteen footers that fall onto the boat like walls.

Sometimes, to elude his terror, he tries his old trick of talking with Picasso. It doesn't work. Instead he hears his sister's "Give *you* a break?" Once, something he'd forgotten came to mind. He was twelve or thirteen, working part time in Sam Berman's jewelry store. Someone had come in to return an engagement ring. Sam was refunding the money when the man started shouting that it was nothing but a no-good Jew ring off a no-good Jew dealer and not fit for a white woman's hand. Sam stood pale and tight lipped. And after the man had left, he turned to him and the salesgirl and, with a smile, explained that probably this man had proposed and been rejected. That was all he said about it. In retrospect, Sam's smiling excuse had been as awful as the bigotry. In retrospect, it reminds him of himself with Roy Higgs.

The bow lifts into a wave and furrows under. A hand of water punches his face. It is a strange vision: the black night and the sea blinding him with its drench of solid white. And holding the boat into the coming waves knowing he is Roy's educated sharecropper. He terrifies himself, a man who works to find excuses for his life as a sharecropper and when his wife quietly points out he is acting like a—like a sharecropper, of course—he beats her. This sea, by comparison, holds no terror. It is what it is. But he is like the sea become land, like earth that actually is gas and fire. He has worked since sixteen to know nothing about himself. He doesn't even know where he's going now, but he believes he'll know when he gets there. The pump is good and there's plenty of fuel.

Waves smash inboard, blinding him, an endless drench. The bandaging is peeled off his arm. There's too much to pay attention to without thinking of why he's loaded on so many bad anchors and extra chain. Between incoming waves, the rain over the windshield drives enough salt from his eye to let him peer down onto the lit compass. He holds the direction north-northwest. He's made twenty, even thirty, miles through this batter. What good is selling the boat if Kate hates him, if Mary Ann hates him? Mickey keeps insisting he hit Bob simply to defend his mother. But then Mickey went home. Where did *he* go? He quit baseball in college because the game reminded him of the playoff day when he made his father kill himself; that is, turn into that thing out at the Sunset Home, that religious Xerox.

Raeburn ducks under the breaking wave and comes up spitting salt. He's an asshole: it wasn't baseball's fault. He's Roy Higgs Jr.'s sharecropper; he's an asshole's asshole. The boat keeps getting battered and keeps coming back for more. *The Mary Ann.* Mary Ann stuck by him until he showed her he wasn't the *him* she'd stuck by. The one thing he owns that isn't Roy's is the boat. So it makes sense, *his boat and his bad anchors.* And he'll know when he gets there, wherever there is. The boat surfs down a wave and lifts as easily as on a sunny day. He raises his head to lick the rain. Eleanor was so angry when he'd asked her to give him a break. He'll give them a break. He's broken Mary Ann's jaw because she was decent and honorable. The boat crests another wave and slides sideways down its back slope, staggering. He could change its name to *Le Bateau d'Ivre.* Another boat was the *Bateau Lavoir.* Nothing was wrong in studying French when he was studying the Cubists: it was giving up baseball that was wrong. It was giving up himself to something inside him that was dead. His father is what was dead inside him. And his mother, though that is unknown and is his terror. He should have coached baseball. At U Miami or Turtle Key High, or Little League. Instead, after walking the mangroves north of town as the storm began, he'd hurried back to the pile of blue and orange anchor boxes and known what to do, loaded them onto the boat with extra line and shackles and put out to sea. Yet, last thing, seeing how hard the wind was blowing and the coconut trees around, he rushed from window to window double X-ing them with masking tape in case the coconuts shot off the trees like cannonballs. Saving Roy's property, a white trash sharecropper to the last.

Raeburn tells himself this isn't a real hurricane. There's not much to fear out here. He re-points the boat into the waves, wanting to be logical. As he understands the calculus, the water for the most is staying still; the waves are merely amplitudes at frequency. What is movement, apart from the boats, is the north wind beating and batting and pock-marking the water's surface. He brings up his wrist, reads five after midnight. If he'd stuck at baseball, only one or two years in the majors would have paid ten times over for Kate's college education. He smiles against the soaking wave. The gusts are, at most, sixty. The boat goes skiing, goes sideways, snowplows. The sores under his right forearm make a dotted, deChirico line up to the time on his wrist, twelve twenty-five.

He hears chimes under the storm, like far off mirrors being broken. But there are no shoals up here. Then the sound is the clank of cowbells, as if a sad soaked herd stood out here. Nothing is here. He throttles back, peering. A black wall rises. He spins the wheel and props himself at the side of the console to fend off with his feet. The boat slides right for the sheer wall and then a wave lifts it away and Raeburn looks up and sees the superstructure lights. He throttles down and lets the wind take him astern where in the ship's lights he reads:

MAID OF ORLEANS

GULF GEOPHYSICS

NEW ORLEANS, LA.

He smiles open-mouthed. Coastal Oil's survey ship is riding out the night on storm anchors. He laughs and feels the rain in his mouth. To have found with such sure sharecropper's instinct his way back to Roy! He yells, "I told you I'd know when I got there." Even if someone were on deck, he couldn't be heard. He feels the panic vibratos climb his chest. He couldn't be seen. He and his fine boat are no more than flotsam from the hulking ship. It isn't his fault. He thinks of all he has to do, and he calms down.

He brings the *Mary Ann* up under the stern of the *Maid of Orleans* for protection, and he sets to work. He's able to unpack two anchors before he has to again bring the *Mary Ann* alee of the survey ship. He repeats this two by two, until all the anchors are in a galvanized heap before the empty boxes, some of which have blown to sea. Then he goes forward to the bow locker, stops to re-position the boat, and he pulls back to the console the ends of the stainless steel chain and nylon line. As he works he sings out "Mary Ann" and "Maid of Orleans" as a work chant. Sometimes the words change to "Joan of Arc" and "Roy Higgs, Jr." When all the chain and line are amidships, he takes a shackle from the box under the console and unscrews its pin, at the same time moving the wheel and throttle to align the boat. He chants "Mary Ann" and "Give me a break." After he's opened ten shackles, he puts one through a link near an end of the chain, takes up an anchor and slips its ring through the shackle and re-screws the pin. In this way, realigning the boat, singing his chanteys, he fastens all ten anchors. He finds pleasure in this work, especially having to keep the boat in place behind the ship's stern, out of the worst of the sea. He's always had good hand-eye coordination. He could see the fastball all the way, knew the split second when the slider sliced down so that he could step in with his weight behind the bat and swing straight through. His clothes are clinging to him in a way that makes no sense, so it's logical to take them off: stone gray tee shirt and shoes and jeans and underpants, all the while working the boat under the stern. He takes off his wristwatch and puts it in the lock-up compartment. For some minutes he stands shivering at the wheel. Then he stops feeling cold.

He looks at his wet arms and chest and stomach. He still has a good body; his body hasn't let him down, only his coward's heart. He thinks he owes his body not to let it wash up, chewed and bloated, in the mangroves. He fixes two boat fenders in reef knots to an end of the nylon line, as floats. He brings up the boat again, and then he takes the end of the anchor chain and end of the line and decides on a bowline. There is some satisfaction even now in being able to come up with the right knot, a simple and secure attachment. All his life fixed to the wrong ones, except Mary Ann and Kate who he's beaten off. The last knot is obvious. He turns a three-foot loop onto a slipknot a few feet along from the anchor chain. He brings the boat back up again and starts to put anchors over the side. One and two and three and four. At the eighth, the chain starts to run, so he brings it inboard and hooks this anchor onto the gunwale. He checks the slipknot for loose ends. "Loose ends" is funny.

Everything is funny now, salt water in his singing mouth. Someone will see the fenders at the end of the line, tomorrow. Or whenever. He drops the slipknot over his head and draws it tight up under his arms. He doesn't like the feel of the nylon across the top of his chest, but you can't have everything. He looks down. His stomach muscles are still good. He brings the boat up one last time and drops the eighth anchor overboard. And the ninth. The chain goes taut. He says "Goodbye." It isn't his fault. It's her fault that he has to do this. He hates her. He lifts off the last anchor. He hates her. Who? He hates Roy. It isn't fair. He sits on the gunwale, swings his legs over and lets the anchor go. The chain bumps over and down. It jumps, it bangs over his sore arm and he screams and laughs in the pain. He knows it's stupid worrying about pain with the chain leaping over the side of the rolling boat. He sings his chantey. Picasso is singing with him, pointing to the anchor boxes, an orange and blue cubist portrait of his Kate; orange planes of her hair, blue cheekbones, her anchor eyes.

Raeburn shouts, "Kate," and he grabs at the chain but it slips faster. He tips backwards into the boat and grabs for the chain. He catches the last of it, and it yanks him to his feet at the gunwale and jerks his arms at their sockets but he can't hold on. He lets go, lunging at a cleat and a link slips on and stops it. He gulps air and looks from the slipknot to the chain not knowing which to go for. The cleat rips off from the boat and the chain shoots out, and he's pulling at the knot and watching the line fly away at his feet. He forces himself to look away from the line at the knot, and he loosens it. He slips the line over his head, and it snaps and flies past his face and burns over his sore arm and whips off. The fenders hit the back of his head and he goes down into the anchor boxes.

They feel soft. He hugs the boxes. He says "Mary Ann" and lifts his head and an incoming wave buries him in white darkness.

Raeburn comes to and goes back to Turtle Key. The sea is slate and purple, shot with white. The boat flies before the wind like sea scud. He's put on only his tee shirt and underpants, but he doesn't feel cold until he's back at his dock tying the boat off on the moor whips. Upstairs over the store, he strips, dries, wraps himself in a blanket and opens a bottle of tequila to get warm. He sits at the table until the bottle is finished. Then he gets to sleep and wakes up, remembering that Mickey has been there and that he's told Mickey about his suicide attempt and made him promise not to mention it. He drinks five glasses of water at the bathroom tap and sits back at the table looking at the box he's brought up from the boat, at the oilskin wrapping the gun. He is going to join their protest, SPOIL, not just to get back in their good graces but because, of course, they've been right. What is the worst that can happen: that he'll loose his failed business? That Kate will have to work her way through college and take loans like a million other kids? He knows he's still drunk but he's thinking straight. He can work for the downtown marina and start coaching baseball part time. He can give Roy a hard time over oil exploration.

He looks for dry clothes and finds them all dirty. He'll go home and get them from the laundry and not disturb anyone. He gets dressed and takes the gun in its oilskin and slips it through his belt, to leave it home for Mary Ann and Kate now that they're alone there. When he gets into the pickup, he knows he's drunk and decides to drive very, very carefully. There are no other cars on the road. The wind has dropped and he's doing between ten and fifteen miles an hour. He turns off Gulf Drive into Pine Shores and sees how neatly and sweetly the houses curve around the streets. He has taught Kate as a toddler half her alphabet by cycling her around Pine Avenue: Alamanda Drive, Barracuda Drive, their street Coral Drive, and Dorado, Everglades and Flying Fish, right to Marlin at the end. The Florida developer's alphabet of old

Roy's first housing tract. Built twice as well as the mall junk Roy Jr. throws up.

He drives down Coral Drive, silent now in its wet wind noise, the houses snug, some with boards up or with windows taped. He is, as the bubbas put it, drunk some. He parks. He supposes he is bubba some. But he's careful not to slam the pickup door. To think he's almost killed himself makes his feet tingle. And now he's here with a good plan, a little drunk and stealing home. Just steal in and get clean clothes and steal away. It seems years since he was out in the storm behind *The Maid of Orleans*. His hand shakes as he turns the key. And now he's inside in the dark and moving quietly through the hall past the stairs. He sees in the living room's nightlight, Kate's arm dangling over the sofa. She must have fallen asleep reading.

He takes three soft steps to see his girl and finds he's looking down at her legs spread over the shoulders of a kneeling, naked man. Kate looks up, says, "Oh my god!" and pushes the man's head from her. She hugs a pillow to her; the young man is saying "What the hell?" He sees Raeburn and springs up and at the same time reaches down for his clothes. He stops half bent over and points. It's Bob Davis, Raeburn sees, straightening and pointing at him. The boy's pale condom sags.

Raeburn is saying, "What? What?" as Bob points at him. Bob's mouth moves without sound. Then out comes "Please, don't. Please, I love Kate with all my heart."

Raeburn sees Bob is pointing to his belt. He holds the gun in his hand, amazed. He says, "This?" looking from the forty-five over to Bob.

Kate moves between them, in her slip. "Dad, for god's sake, get out of here!"

Raeburn says, "You thought... No." He picks up Bob's trousers and hands them around Kate to Bob. Bob takes them, scoops his shoes and socks from the floor and runs from the room with his head bent, as if ducking bullets.

Kate says, "What the hell are you doing here? Will you put that down!" She follows Bob out. Raeburn hears them talking at the front door. It shuts. Kate comes back wet with rain, clutching her arms about her so that her freckled shoulders are pulled forward. They look bony and delicate.

He says, "I snuck in for clean clothes."

"You shouldn't be here and you know it."

"I've had a hard night, with the storm and checking the boat and things."

"Right. Will you please go now? And put that gun away."

Raeburn sets it and its oilcloth down on a chair. "For you and Mary Ann. I thought—"

"I don't care what you thought. You don't want to wake Mom, do you?"

He goes to the door and says. "Look, I like Bob. And I'm going to join that anti-oil group."

"Sure, Dad. You should sleep it off. And for your information, Bob and I plan to live together our second year at Miami." She closes the door.

Outside, he thinks that what he wanted to do was to have camomile tea with Kate. In the pickup, he rests his cheek against the steering wheel. He tells himself it's been a pretty good night: he has his life, his daughter, and maybe a chance for his wife. But something in him knows it's not any good, and slowly and steadily he bangs his head against the wheel.

Chapter Seven _____

LIKE OTHER WHITE LIBERALS, I have prejudices about black people. Like other white jazz musicians, I know one of them: I like them. They've created the music I love. In 1993, I was probably the only Turtle Key white man openly going with a Turtle Key black woman. Charlene Varez and I had been seeing each other for over a year. The trouble was that Tony Varez, my bass player and her cousin, seemed suddenly to have noticed and taken offence at our relationship. There were other problems in my relations with Charlene, but they don't concern this story.

The night it came to a head was the first of July, a Thursday. I remember the date because—and I'm not going to analyze this, either—it was the night I began my affair with Anita Higgs. That day even began dramatically. I came into the club at three in the afternoon to work at the piano. No sooner did I play a few notes than Frank Edrich came out of the office and asked me to come back there with him, something he had to tell me. The rain was coming down so hard on the tin roof that he had to raise his voice.

I said I'd come in after my piano work. Frank said it had to be right then. Well, Frank is as laid back a gent as I know, so I figured I'd better go. In the office, I asked what was wrong.

"Nothing. Roy Higgs came in for lunch with some of his high rolling cronies and stuck around afterwards to talk to me. He said would I be interested in selling the club to him. Just straight out, like that. Since I'd never given it a thought, I gave him a wiseass answer. Sure, I said, and I picked a crazy number—I'll sell it to you for fifteen million dollars. Mickey, the man didn't bat an eyelash. He said, 'Okay, I'll think about it.' Then he slapped my back bubba fashion and left. Fifteen million. You have twenty percent of this place. You see what kind of money that is?"

"I can do the math. Do you want to sell the place?"

"No. Especially not to Roy."

"If someone else offered you that money, some philanthropist?"

"I don't want to sell. Do you?"

"Not me. I like it here. It's a good gig. We're doing alright, aren't we?"

"Yes we are. You know we are. We're making, as they say, a nice living."

"Good. So I can get back to the piano, and we don't have to think of this anymore."

"Absolutely. But I had to tell you."

"Of course, Frank. Thanks."

I went back and played the piano for an hour, and about ten times a minute, for sixty minutes, I thought, "Three million. Three million dollars." And I bet Frank in the office was thinking, "Twelve million. Twelve million dollars." But when I got home and calmed down, I knew I wanted the club, not the money. Besides, I had money enough. So did Frank, and I figured that was his thinking, too. Sometimes there's a sort of default virtue in laziness.

101

The club was packed that night, though the Fourth of July weekend hadn't begun. Maybe the constant wind and rain had driven everyone slightly out of their heads and homes into the club, or into anything that passed for distraction. And the Spongers was packed with hard drinkers, from whom I don't exclude my trio. What I was doing, pouring us out the Laphroaig from my private stock, was trying to cool Tony out. It had no such effect. His playing was too furiously hot. All his subtlety was gone. At the bar's back corner, end of the first set, I again offered the bottle. Tony said, "Why not?" Ben Niles gave his usual, "Just one finger, man," holding his index finger vertically. I poured three heavy drinks. The club's multicolored lights reflected on Tony's elegant shaved head and Ben's bumpy bald one. Ben toasted, "To summer vacation. Man, month more, I'm outa here to somewhere *unflat*, unsweaty, too. Smokies, maybe, or up the Adirondacks. You, Tony?"

"I'm gonna make it up to New York, hear the sounds, sit in some."

"You Mick?"

"I haven't thought about it." This wasn't exactly true. Since the night before, I'd been considering getting away from old TK.

Ben said, "Hey, before you got back here, we were talking ostinato. I was telling our young talent, here, don't scorn it, see how he could work ostinato, make it his own."

Ben was doing his diplomatic best. I watched the smoke snaking up from the cigarette on Tony's lip. Tony said, "Ostinato's okay behind a second-rate pianist. But Mickey's up to my free-form chording." He stared at me through his smoke.

Ben said, "Listen, genius boy, Miles said how he slowed way down so's someone other than Diz and Bird could hear what he was doing. Miles Davis, man, not just some candyass nigger playing Mason funerals hereabouts."

Tony said, "Well, shit," and kept looking at me. I looked

around for someone I knew. I feel uncomfortable, at the best of times, when black people in my hearing say "nigger," and this wasn't the best of times. I didn't see anyone I knew.

I said, "Don't knock funeral gigs, Ben. That's how Fats Navarro got started in Key West."

Tony said, "You're not actually coming in on my side of an argument, for once, are you, boss?"

There was no avoiding it. I said, "No, I don't think so."

Tony said, "Good."

I offered the bottle.

Tony said, "Yeah, don't mind."

Ben said, "Yessir. They call it a 'fluff-up'."

Tony said, "Speaking of fluff, it true you're boning my cousin Charlene?"

"We've been seeing each other for a year. It's no secret."

"Yes. Well, what can I say, man? It's your whiskey, your trio, your club." Tony was smiling behind his cigarette fume.

"I don't want your deference, fake or real. Just say what's on your mind."

"What's on my mind is how you're using your position to take advantage of Charlene, and of her family which, yeah, includes me."

I swallowed a mouthful of Scotch. "Jesus, let me just separate out some of the craziness you've loaded in there. What you mean, I take it, is I'm white."

"Hey, do my uncle and aunt approve of this?"

"I don't know. I haven't met them yet. We haven't sat down to share a bowl of gefilte chitlins, or whatever we're supposed to do." This was also not the case. I hadn't met them, but I knew they didn't approve. Of course, I had to go on. "What are you suggesting, that I turn up and say, 'Hi, Mr. and Mrs. Varez, I'm thirty-six-year-old Mickey Berman and I'd like your permission to date your thirty-two-year-old, divorced daughter Charlene?'"

Tony took a step so that he stood very close to me. His cigarette smoke was going up into my eye. He said, "Fuck your sarcasm, man. What you're saying is you're free, white, and over twenty-one. But Charlene isn't. Yes. It would be decent if you put your free white face round there to introduce yourself."

"I'd like to and I will when Charlene wants me to." This was the worst lie, inasmuch as the night before, Charlene had walked out. That is, she'd been offered a great teaching job in Atlanta and asked me if I knew a reason—"a good, long-term, committed sort of reason," she'd said—why she shouldn't go. And I'd looked into her eyes and said no, she should take the job. So I felt bad, but it still seemed important to hold my ground with Tony.

Then Ben's bald head appeared between us. "Tony, man, tell you what's good an decent is you take your black fool face out from business that ain't yours."

Tony tilted his head and looked past Ben, at me. "I'll tell it to you straight: I hate you going with Charlene not because of the color of white skin but because it's going to bring her lots of unhappiness and her family, my family, lots of unhappiness. Because that's how it always is."

The unhappiness had already come about, though I thought not from color differences but from certain man and woman differences. Still, I didn't have to watch Spike Lee films to know Tony was right. I said, "I hear you. Now I'll tell you something straight, as a musician and leader of the trio, and, if you want, as your boss. I'm working with a young bass player who has big talent, who actually has the ear and technique to be seriously good. But his anger is fucking up his music."

"And I have nothing to be angry about?"

"You have the whole world to be angry about. But get it working *for* your music, not like a bomb that blows it to pieces."

"Shit, Ben, we got another white man telling a black man he's too angry."

"Wait a second. You're right, I'm white, I have money, I don't know a thing about your anger. What I know is music. You're angry? Make it music, like Mingus did, like Donny Wells does." I'd played with Donny in New York, and Tony was in awe of him.

Tony stubbed out his cigarette and lit another. He took half a drag and crushed it out into the ashtray.

I said, "Ben, how would *you* feel if, say, I was going out with your sister?"

Ben scratched the white hair over his ear. "Only have brothers. But, say you was gay and one of them was? I wouldn't mind."

"Thanks a lot."

"Mind, I wouldn't want you *marryin* my brother."

While we were smiling, I walked away.

I sat in the office armchair wondering how long I was going to be able to hold on to Tony, who even playing like this, was better than any other bass player I could get and keep around here. Which made me think of how cocaine hadn't been the cause of my leaving New York: I took more and more coke because I couldn't keep working hard enough at my music to stay in that top jazz scene. Coke was the excuse for my lack of a real artist's temperament. And these thoughts, I knew, would lead to missing the cocaine and drinking too much whiskey as a substitute, so I went back out to the club thinking to begin the second set early, start off by playing solo piano until the others joined me.

Coltrane's "Giant Steps" was coming from the sound system when I saw Anita. She was dressed in a splendid vanilla suit. We took each other's hands and I bent to kiss her cheek, but she turned her head so that we kissed on the lips. A light kiss on the lips, but nothing neighborly about it. I knew. She knew.

She said, "You haven't answered my phone messages, you rat."

"I've been busy with the end of an affair."

"That beautiful Charlene Varez? Poor you."

She gave me a mock maternal hug. Her jacket swung forward and I saw she was naked beneath.

"I like your suit, Anita."

"Double breasted."

"I'll say. So how's Roy: surviving the turtle sanctuary publicity?"

"Naturally. He called in lots of favors. Also, Roy's great talent is swimming through shit."

"… and coming out clean," I finished.

"That or going in so covered in it that no one can tell the difference." She held onto my hand. "Roy says you should join our table. He told me to say if you don't, he'd rob the joint."

"He's trying to buy it. Maybe it comes to the same thing, with him. If he really wants to scare a pianist, he should threaten to break his fingers."

"Not these lovely fingers." She squeezed my hand. We stood very close, in the crowd out from the bar.

"I'm going to start the set. I'll join you afterwards."

"Please."

I knew she wasn't asking about me at her husband's table. I said, "No question."

But no sooner did I signal Ben and Tony than the gloom and jitters came on me again. Why hadn't I grown up and set up home with Charlene? Or join her in Atlanta and play piano there? Could I really be hip and a hick at the same time?

A few numbers into the set, I relaxed. And by the middle of the set, in a moderate paced blues, I noticed that Tony was listening, playing a lightly swinging bass with only half again more notes than necessary. Later, in a slow "My Funny Valentine," Tony laid down a sad contrapuntal line that had Ben and me nodding to each other. Then, at the end, when I asked, "One more?" Tony nodded: "Yeah, let's do it, man."

I leaned forward to the mike. "We'd like to close this set with

'Stella by Starlight'." I looked at Ben. "Our drummer has just informed me that it's in the key of B flat. Let's hear it for our drummer, the great Ben Niles!" There was loud applause. A good audience. "Let's have another round for his finally figuring out it's in B flat." Ben gave himself a drum roll. This wasn't the first time we'd done this. You work with someone for years, you work out little gags, *shticks.*

I waited for the club to quiet. Then, without intro, I played the first four bars on my own, very simply. I've always been drawn to "Stella," the way its resolutions are so tentative, unstable, tipping over, falling down and then climbing back towards further elusive resolution. I thought, as Ben and Tony came in on my nod, it was a musical equivalent of Keats's "Grecian Urn;" the beauty of reaching for something, of yearning. I heard myself getting into the music, hands, ears and feeling joined deep. We played it through once, I nodded double tempo, and began to improvise.

The music: I forgot to know the three thousand reasons why I couldn't play so well, develop melodic lines that long, find such left-hand patterns of rhythm in the chord progressions, urging my right hand deeper inside the melody until not my hands but my whole body was playing piano, moving past that to where piano played me, and, finally, to where there was no me, no piano, only music, only the music. I wanted this forever, but wanting was the knowledge of impossibility, and on that yearning I had to stop and have Tony take his solo.

I first couldn't hear him because my head was still in my own solo. Then because of the applause, the whole club on its feet, clapping, whistling, yelling. I was happy, sad it wasn't New York, happy it happened at all, this is so seldom. Then I heard Tony. I heard him becoming a great bass player. Right there, bending close to his axe, big fingered hands flying, resting, stroking its neck and its belly, his huge technique serving the music rather than shouting "Watch this!" to some skeptic honky in his head.

Then Ben and I came in again through the applause, original tempo, played it through once more and ended. Big, long applause, the best of it the quick looks between the three of us. There aren't words for this. What could I say, that the muse had landed for ten minutes? It's stupid like that. I announced the break, told them to order lots of drinks and we'd be back for our third and final set around one A.M.

Tony shook my hand and said, "Thank you." Wonders unceasing. Maybe in return I should have told him he needn't worry about Charlene and me, but that seemed too much a downer. I made my way through the backslapping, handshaking crowd to Roy's table, where four people had just left, backing away, as if in the presence of royalty.

Roy saw me and stood. He was wearing a black striped seersucker suit and white silk tee shirt. He looked tipsy, tubby and unhip, despite, or maybe because of, trying.

"Mickey, my friend, my buddy. Great solo. Anita knows jazz more than me, and she says it was great. I mean more than I do."

I shook his hand and sat where he put me, between the two of them. Anita kissed my cheek. "That was wonderful."

"Sometimes it happens."

Roy said, "Have some of this sodee-pop." He pulled a bottle of Dom Perignon from the wooden ice tub. Three empties lolled behind it.

"I'm drinking Scotch, thanks. But you go on; you're making Frank happy." I saw Peggy, the waitress, and asked her to bring my Laphroaig. Roy filled their glasses.

He said, "I'm making Frank happy by seriously considering the ridiculous price he asked for this place."

"Named, not asked."

"Boys, no business, please." Anita put her hand on the side of my thigh.

"This isn't business. This is your husband talking dirty.

I know, Roy. Frank and I discussed it. We're honored, but we decline."

"What's your stake, Mickey, two percent?"

"Twenty, but that's not the point, either."

Roy drank off his champagne. Under my jacket, Anita's fingers slid over the top of my thigh.

Roy said, "I can see, then, I'm also going to have to take seriously some damn fantasy price *you* name for your father's building."

Anita said, "Roy, honey, I asked you nicely. But how come you call that his father's building when you don't call Higgs construction your father's business?"

Peggy set down a bottle of whiskey, a glass, and a bowl of ice. She asked if everyone was all right.

Roy said, "Jest hunkey dory, sunshine." He turned to Anita. "Just whose side are you on, here?"

"Why, on Mickey's, of course. Even if you weren't so condescending, moonshine."

Roy put his hands up in mock surrender. Several people took it as a signal and waved back at him, so he smiled and waved back at them.

I said, *"Noblesse oblige."*

"You had better believe that," Roy said, shifting from Bubba to his Chapel Hill mode. "Are you going anywhere this summer, Mickey, or do you plan to sit around at your piano here, entertaining the *hoi polloi*?"

"I'll go somewhere. I haven't decided, yet."

Anita leaned across me. "Roy, wouldn't it be wonderful if Mickey came with us? Mickey, we're taking this great trip, through the Yucatan and Belize into Guatemala, north of Tikal, where we'll camp. But comfortably. Roy gets to watch his hummingbirds and I poke around Mayan ruins. Please come. It'll be such fun. Won't it be such fun, Roy, honeybun?"

I'd seen that one second look of his on other people once or twice before, in New York clubs: a flash of cold rage which convinced you the man was capable of murder. But I'd never seen it emerge from so soft a face as Roy's. Then it was gone and he was smiling. "Of course, great idea. I'm sorry I didn't think of it myself. Come on, Mickey. I promise you won't have gone camping with such good wines before."

Anita said, "Please?" Her hand under the table moved over my cock.

I said, "All right. Thanks, I'd really like to," and we began toasting the trip and talking details. I thought it was the answer to all my blues and jitters. I didn't know I was way out of my league. I didn't have a clue.

Chapter Eight _____

ANITA AND ROY LEFT TOWN after the Fourth. Anita and I were still, technically, not lovers. I'd arranged to meet them in the Yucatan at the end of July. I'd dedicated the intervening four weeks to the trio and to helping Bill get back together with his family. "Dedicated" is an exaggeration: what I did was keep the trio and Bill in mind. With the trio, this meant extra afternoon rehearsals and added concentration when we played at night. Tony wasn't good, he was astoundingly good. When Ben asked me what I thought the chances of Tony's returning to the gig once he got up to New York, I said, "Conservatively, zero."

And I helped convince Bill to agree to Mary Ann's demand that he start counseling before she'd meet him again. He found someone in Naples. After his first session, I asked how it went. He said, "Like at the dentist's, without Novocain." I told him that was good. I suppose I should have spent time with Kate, taken her out for lunch, or something. I was her godfather, but only the Christmas and birthday gift kind.

I keep referring to the weather, but Bill's story, as I've come to think of it, wouldn't have happened but for the weather. Early July continued to be strange. Days of hot wild storms followed by rainless days of hot, deep gray. We started to get used to gray. If the sun came out, it did so in a morning or evening corner of the sky like a pale yellow stain. It was on one of those big stormy nights, off Fort Meyers, the seventh or eighth of July, that Coastal Oil's main pipeline broke and, despite Roy's assurances to Dee Dee Prentice at the Turtle Sanctuary, poured nearly two million gallons of Bonita crude into the Gulf of Florida, where the winds and currents began to push it south. Then the weather broke. Clear cooler days came down from the north, cooler in a TK summer meaning the mid eighties.

That next weekend, I gave one of my Sunday brunches: lox, whitefish, bagels, grits, mint juleps—what Myra Edrich, Frank's wife, once dubbed "bringing the Bowery to the Confederacy." The purpose of this one was bringing Mary Ann to Bill in a setting she'd feel safe. Kate was no problem. Bill's joining SPOIL had brought her around, as well as that closeness about dads and their daughters everyone tells me about. I'd left a phoned invitation at Groves Island for the Higgses, even though I knew Roy was shuttling his ass off between Fort Meyers, Tallahassee, and Washington as part of Coastal's frantic damage control. And I knew that Anita was in New Orleans, because we spoke twice a day. She phoned me late morning because she assumed that's when jazz musicians were just getting up. I pretended I was taking these sexy wake-up calls in bed. Most often, I was at the piano, or doing some housework, or reading the *New York Times*. At night, I phoned during a break and learned, among other things, more of how Roy was doing to the public what he wasn't doing to her.

The usual crowd came to the brunch: the Edrichs, Ben and Barbara Niles, Tony Varez who'd brought a wonderful looking tall woman named Venetia. Tony was maybe too charming. He said he'd heard I'd split up with Charlene and despite our disagreement he was sorry for me. I nodded. I put his condescension down to youth. Others were there singly, in couples, in clans: Rodriguez's and James's, Collins's and Katz's. Charlie Styles from the bank was there: I'd set up a credit line loan for Bill, so I thought it might be good for Charlie to see him socially. Kate Raeburn was there with her boyfriend Bob Davis. Kate wasn't a great beauty, but she was fine looking—tall and athletic with wonderful reddish blond hair.

Kate asked, "I heard this term on the radio: 'stride piano.' What's that?"

I put my left hand on a table and moved it. "There it is, a striding, walking back and forth of chords along down there."

She said, "Could you show me on the piano?"

I said, "Not now. If I did, everyone would start requesting numbers and my hosting would be shot. But come to the club some afternoon, and I'll show you. I promise." That was some promise.

Eleanor Smith, Bill's sister, was there. What Eleanor lacked in physical charm she more than made up for in rudeness. Her first comment, as I greeted her, was, "Okay, Mickey, how many women do you have stashed in the penthouse these days?" "None," I said. Her second comment was, "Bull dickey! You screw anything that moves in a skirt." I think I said, "Charming." Her third comment came later on, when we passed each other in front of a painting. "Christ, Diego Rivera. I always forget how rich you are." She'd said this each time she'd been there before. I said, "Sam bought that in the Forties, so it wasn't that expensive. But, yes, I guess I have a lot more money than you. Is this a proposal, Eleanor?" She said, "I'm envious, not masochistic." Then she asked for a donation to help bring Coastal to court to get punitive damages for the oil spill. Writing the check, I told her it wasn't so much the good cause as her diplomacy that got me to contribute. I don't know why I keep trying with people who aren't nice, or who just don't like me.

The oil spill was of course the big topic of conversation that day. Would it reach us? Would it break up, would they have to fire it? I was more interested in my matchmaking, rematchmaking. When Mary Ann arrived, I had Bill just happen to be in the front hall with me, and after a bad silence in which I thought Mary Ann might bolt back into the elevator, Bill said hello. Mary Ann just looked at the floor. I left them to whatever might happen, which turned out to be nothing at all. So when we started eating, I grabbed Mary Ann's hand and Bill's hand and had them sit either side of me.

Finally, Mary Ann said, "How many kinds of smoked fish do you have here?"

"Smoked salmon, smoked sturgeon, smoked whitefish, smoked sable. I just explained to Kate's friend, Bob, that sable was a fish as well as a fur. I also have creamed herring, which isn't smoked and which is being eaten only by me."

Bill said, "What about this slick?"

I said, "I don't know. But what about this weather? Why don't we take advantage of it and get out on the boat for an afternoon?"

Bill said, "Our boat?"

I said, "Your boat. I don't have a boat. I'll provide the picnic and drink. Mary Ann?"

She said, "Oh, you meant me, too? It's great how you just assumed I'd want to be with him."

I said, "Him's name is Bill, and I assumed nothing. But I am doing my damnedest to give you a pretext or do I mean an excuse for meeting. It's been weeks and weeks. And I'd be the chaperone and/or the referee and general friend to both, or the chief arbiter and ombudsman. Yessiree."

Bill said, "I could close the store Friday."

She said, "You, close Roy's investment?"

He said, "Our store."

She said, "I'll think about it.

I saw she was impressed by Bill's new attitude. I said, "And the weather's supposed to hold."

I was right about the weather. My idea was simply to bring the two of them together in something less than a crowd. Maybe if we hadn't gone out in the boat that day things wouldn't have been so bad. Maybe they would have. What happened was that by Friday the slick had drifted down past Turtle Key and was headed right for Loggerhead Key, part of the National Marine Sanctuary of South Florida. Questions were being raised in Congress, as well as in Tallahassee, and the Coast Guard and Navy and Marine Patrol, in conjunction with Coastal Oil, had promised a clean burn-off if the slick held and weather conditions were good. Kate was going out in Bob Davis's boat as part of the flotilla monitoring the burn-off. The firing of the slick was going to be some time in the afternoon. I suggested we have our boating picnic en route and meet up with the other boats off Loggerhead. Bill said he'd pick me up at eleven-thirty at the town dock outside the club, where I was having the kitchen make our picnic. He actually said he and Mary Ann would pick me up, so I assumed things were on the mend with them.

I was outside the club before eleven-thirty. At noon, I brought the picnic back in to the cold room and called TK Marine. No one there. I yakked to Terrence at the bar for the next forty minutes hoping Bill and Mary Ann hadn't started fighting and split up again. Far from it. I heard Bill's boat hooting at a quarter to one, brought out the picnic and asked what had happened. Bill said, "Sorry, we got held up," looking at the containers he was putting into the cooler. Mary Ann studied the labels on the champagne. I figured what embarrassed them was what had held them up. Making love. I couldn't help smiling. This was going to haunt all three of us.

We went out to the Gum Keys. The winds were middling but seemed to keep changing direction. The sea was a shifty two to three foot chop. Bill thought the burn-off might well be cancelled: he didn't see how the slick could stay together in this weather. We anchored in the salt river channel that essed through Big Gum Key. I was very pleased with myself; I'd helped bring Bill and Mary Ann back together. The way they looked at each other as they passed the plate of shrimp or when I toasted "new beginnings." New beginnings, Jesus. We started too late and we stayed too long.

Bill went for Loggerhead at high speed. Before she saw the island, Mary Ann made out the boats through her binoculars. They were heading back towards us. Ten minutes later we were in among seven or eight boats flying purple and yellow monitor flags. Bill said Bob Davis's boat wasn't there. He brought the boat alongside the boat of Kate's friend Margaret Jack. I put out fenders, Mary Ann threw a line to the crowd in the boat. She asked Margaret what we'd missed. Margaret said it was a joke. When they got out there, it was called off because it was too gusty and changing direction too much to fire. She said the last she'd seen of Kate and Bob, Bob's boat was at the west end of Loggerhead, seeing how close the slick was coming. Then the Coast Guard had come and said the firing was off until tomorrow and the slick was going to miss the key. They would have gone off with some of the other boats making back up along the Glades.

When Margaret cast off, Bill said, "We've come this far. We could go on and get a look at the slick off Loggerhead then cut east and catch Kate and Bob, or at least catch sunset along the Glades."

Mary Ann said, "Let's do it. You've closed the sweatshop. We can make a day of it."

We continued southwest at high speed. Soon Mary Ann made out the key and a string of big ships off to the west. She said, "The biggest ones must be Coastal's clean-up ships. The others must be Navy, Coast Guard and Marine Patrol." Then I made out the long atoll arms of Loggerhead Key. Bill turned to ask what was loose in the stern, but then we heard another thud. There was a flash out past the ships and then another thud. Two balls of smoke lifted like signals.

Bill said, "Sneaky bastards. They said it would be tomorrow to get rid of the monitor boats."

Mary Ann said, "Maybe it was for safety."

Bill said, "That's what they'll say. But it's their own safety, more likely. Coastal will be laughing. No witnesses except that helicopter and that's probably an oil-drilling friendly TV station."

Out before us was another flash, a thud, a smudge of charcoal smoke and a dab of red-orange fire. Then another flash and another, thuds and puffs of smoke and lines of fire on the black sea. And then over miles it looked like flashbulbs going off and turning black over their burning bases. Bill said, "We seem to be the only citizens left out here and all the official boats are busy firing the slick. Why don't we slip into Loggerhead behind them to monitor?"

Mary Ann and I agreed. I said, "Is that how the slick is supposed to burn?"

Mary Ann said, "No. They said it should fire all at once and the smoke should lift right off."

Bill said, "It's these cyclonic gusts. Or the slick has broken up. Or both."

We continued running for the key. I watched the burn-off. The fires showed now as orange waves. The balls of smoke above were flattening down, not lifting. It was like a giant hand was shading in the area over the slick. Mary Ann said, "Kate kept saying she didn't think Coastal's promise of 'clean firing' would work. Why does anyone ever believe these people?"

I said, "Maybe the slick suddenly changed directions and

was going to hit Loggerhead, so they decided to try this."

Bill said, "I'm glad it's us and not Kate and Bob or the other kids out here. Look at that smoke."

He headed for the center of the key, so that its outswung western tip would keep us hidden. Mary Ann looked through her binoculars and said she saw no boats up on the beach. Bill slowed the boat to find the channel in through the reef. We saw the smoke slowly moving towards the key's west end. Mary Ann said, "There's the colony of frigate birds out there." Bill said, "And the big heronries at the southwest." He was working the boat slowly east along the reef line. It was hard to judge the movement of the smoke. If it was moving off, it was doing so imperceptibly, a roiling filthy fleece with thudding and popping from the fires bursting out beneath it. Bill missed the channel and had to turn back west. Then we saw it, the slightly bluer ten-foot swath through the brown-yellow reef water. We went through and came into the lagoon along the beach. Bill picked up speed and went west until we could smell the smoke.

He said, "It's awful. I once walked into an oil fire at the edge of the dump. Disgusting. Should we leave?"

Mary Ann said, "No, we're here." She tied a kerchief bandana style over her nose and mouth. Bill and I did the same with handkerchief bandanas. Bill tilted up the motors, revved, and ran the prow up into the sand. If I didn't look at the smoke, the beach looked as wonderful as ever. Once, Bill had brought me out here to watch Ridley turtles come ashore to lay eggs. But when I turned to where Mary Ann pointed, I saw the smoke at the west of the island had become a volcano. It boiled black, hundreds of feet high. Flames rolled underneath as if from lava.

Bill said, "Someone should stay with the boat. I'll get as close a look as I can without being stupid."

Mary Ann said, "Mickey, you stay. I'll go with Bill."

I said, "I'm not much use with boats."

She said, "All right. But no heroics?"

I said, "Me? Are you kidding?"

We jumped off onto the beach and went west. After a few hundred yards my lips became oily with the smoke through the cloth. After another hundred, the air down my nose was greasy and bitter. I followed Bill's example and bent low into slightly better air. Even behind sunglasses and the pulled-down visor my eyes were tearing. I hated it, but I thought I couldn't just leave him. Bill turned and said he thought we could make it to the salt creek at the western edge where the mangroves began. Then we wouldn't have to take Coastal's word for what the smoke did. I said, "What about the Marine Patrol?" He said, "Let's use our own eyes. I promise we won't do anything stupid." We wiped the smoke grease off our sunglasses. Bill did the same with his binoculars. The air was yellow brown. The thudding had stopped, but the smoke kept rising in an enormous shaking column from the key's western tip. We moved off in a deep crouch to stay in better air. I had a headache. The beach went on forever. I swallowed down vomit and kept my eyes down at my feet. Sand, a broken float, Bill's footsteps, a coil of drift line, seaweed, a smashed blue point crab, turkey wing shells, a helmet sponge. A line of seaweed I crunched for thirty steps, a mangrove root. I looked ahead. Bill was sitting at the edge of the salt creek. I came up and sat beside him.

We could hardly breathe. The air was a ruinous burnt brown. I said, "Are we at the limit of not being stupid?" He said, "Almost. I'll just wade up the creek some, see what I can through these and be back. Five minutes. You stay here or start back." I said okay and Bill wiped his glasses and binoculars and put his rag in his back pocket and went into the creek. I didn't want to be on my own, so I followed him. The creek was only three feet deep but we squatted for the better air and went waist to shoulder high. After a few minutes, the creek narrowed, mangrove roots appeared, branches

119

tunneled the creek. I was set to poke Bill if the smoke got any worse. I couldn't stand it. The creek ran shallower. We duck-walked to keep our heads low. Then we went to our knees on the creek's fine sand. Half the time I had my eyes shut against the burn of the smoking air. Opening them didn't improve things. Bill was stopped ahead. I caught up. He held a dead heron: oil soot smeared its feathers, its eyelids were smoked brown paper. Bill had to bend double to keep his head down and the heron's neck and legs hung impossibly thin and long off his hands. Then I noticed the fish come floating by, mangrove snappers, belly up. Bill hung the heron over some branches. He croaked in my ear: "We're real close to where this opens to thatch palms and sea oats at the southwest point. We'll be able to see what's happened to the bird colonies out there in the high mangroves. And it's just as close back to the beach from there. You okay?" I held my thumb up. Bill turned, looked through his binoculars and turned back. He started to say something, swallowed some air and fell back on the mud bank vomiting. Which was all I needed. I fell onto the other side, pulled off the bandana and watched the vomit come onto the mud in black strings. Bill came across and pointed: "Something's up there." He went on. I put the bandana back on and followed. The water surface was a solid film of soot and oil droplets. I saw something white in the mangroves just ahead of Bill. I made it out when I came up to him. He'd pulled back a mangrove branch and gray tree crabs were running over his hand. The stern of a boat. *My Sunshine*. Turtle Key, FL. Bill pulled himself up above the gunwales. He came down and said, "Thank God. There's no one in there. It's Bob's boat." I said, "Oh, God." I followed Bill along the side of the boat to the bank. A pale sand path ran up from it. We fell back and pulled off the bandanas. They were black brown with oil. Bill said, "This path curves back around to the beach. Kate and Bob will either be at the boat with Mary Ann or around on the south shore." I nodded. Neither of us

120

could stand, we were so sick with oil fumes. We went on our hands and knees and crawled along the path. Hand after hand, I saw as much oil soot as grains of sand. I watched the bottom of Bill's sneakers moving ahead. We were crawling past a low sand slope. Some wind came and I could breathe. Then I was looking at his trouser legs. He was standing by the slope, saying, "Kate? Katie, you quit that." I got to my feet.

Kate was on her side in a bikini with her head tucked under her arms. She was streaked with oil. Bill went to his knees beside her. Her bikini was streaked black like our vomit. I could understand why he wasn't touching her. She was the deadest thing I'd ever seen. Bill kept repeating, "Kate, Kate." It sounded like he was breathing her name in and out. I was shocked dumbstruck. We stayed just like that in the clearing air. Bill kept breathing her name in and out. In the clearness I heard the footsteps turn in from the beach and Mary Ann walked up to Bill on his knees and said, "What are you doing?" And when he turned to her, she slapped the side of his face and knocked him down.

"Kneeling like that like a fool." She was kneeling, talking to her dead daughter. She turned Kate onto her back and brought her arms to her sides. She put her ear to Kate's mouth and looked down her chest. Bill got up and said to no one in particular, "Kate's so dirty." Mary Ann put a hand on Kate's forehead and lifted her chin. She turned Kate's head and put two fingers down Kate's throat and pulled out thick black ropes of vomit. "There it is. Can you imagine? Your father was doing nothing." Bill said, "I hate to see Kate's hair so dirty." Mary Ann straightened Kate's head and pinched her nostrils. She put her mouth over Kate's mouth and blew in and looked down at her chest. She said, "Okay, Katie, let's check it out." She put a hand on Kate's forehead and two fingers under her chin and turned her head back up. I saw her oily finger marks under Kate's hair. She pinched Kate's nostrils and blew into her mouth. She said to her, "Don't worry," and moved her fingers up along her neck. They made slide marks. "Right, okay," she said. She felt over Kate's breastbone and set the heel of her hand there. Bill said, "I understand, but I want to wipe the oil from her hair." He wasn't talking to anyone. Mary Ann put her other hand over her hand on Kate's breastbone and locked fingers. She pushed up and locked her elbows and pressed down and released. "One and two and three and four and," she counted with the pressing. Bill was looking at Kate's hair. Mary Ann said, "And fourteen and fifteen," and she stopped. She went on her knees to Kate's head, tilted back her chin and gave her two breaths of mouth-to-mouth. She looked down Kate's chest for breath and then felt on her neck for a pulse. She moved back on her knees to Kate's chest and set her hands on the breastbone and locked her elbows and began compressing and counting. At fifteen she stopped and moved up to Kate's head for mouth-to-mouth. She felt for her pulse and said, "Right. Your father has to take over because I have to rest for a bit." Mary Ann was slick with sweat. She stared at Bill across Kate. "Can you do that? Do you think you could *do* this single thing? Fifteen times, compress about one and a half to two inches deep and let go and do it again."

Bill came around on his knees to the other side of his dead daughter. Mary Ann placed his hands on Kate's breastbone. It was clear that Bill knew Kate was dead. He locked his fingers and elbows and began. Mary Ann said, "Too deep," the first two times. He said, "Five and six and seven and." He might have thought seeing him do this would bring Mary Ann to her senses. He stopped. Mary Ann checked for Kate's pulse. I tried to think how long it had been since the smoke fell on the island. Half an hour, an hour. We were going to be here forever. Mary Ann would go on and on. She pushed Bill with her hip: "Move." She said, "Katie, it's time you got in the recovery position." Bill said, "The recovery position," to no one. Her hands slid off the oily skin. Bill brought Mary Ann's hand back over Kate's hip and pushed and they got her onto her side. Mary Ann adjusted Kate's head to keep the airway open. She set the arms and legs so that the body wouldn't roll onto its face. She stood and said, "There, Katie. I've done all I can for now. I hear some boats coming."

Bill stood and took the rag from his pocket. He said, "I'd like to clean Kate's hair."

Mary Ann said, "What for? She's dead."

She finally looked at me. "Why don't you be of some use and get to the beach?"

I took off. I ran as though whipped.

Later, returning in the Coast Guard boat with Kate's corpse and Bob Davis's corpse forward under blankets and the three of us in blankets on a side bench, Bill tried to put his arm around Mary Ann and she pushed it away. I tried and she pushed it away. She said, "I figured it out, Mickey. When we were late picking you up it was because we were making… Fucking, because we were fucking. That extra time, that hour and we would have met up with their boat and saved Kate. You know that, Bill? We never would have let her get into that smoke. What Bill and I did was killed her like we made her. We killed her like we made her." We both said, "No, Mary Ann." She shrugged off Bill's arm. She didn't talk anymore except, from time to time, to say, "We killed her like we made her." What was I thinking? Of nothing, of watching the sea, of my brunch and Mary Ann asking me about smoked fish.

Chapter Nine _____

RAEBURN KNOWS THE ROOM IS full of people, but there is a film between him and them. Their images blur and their words muffle. They're ghosts of condolence. He moves through them to the living room window to look out at the cars. The cars may convince him of all the people. Parked cars fill the street all the way to Pine Avenue. He can see Al Jarowski directing traffic and parking cars. Al had come early to the door. He said, "Oh, jeez, Bill, I don't know. I just don't know what. Know what I mean?" He clutched his cop's hat with both hands as if it would blow away or as if he would.

Raeburn looks at the sun shining off the car roofs. Nothing has seemed real except a few minutes when Rita and Dick Davis appeared and he remembered that their child was dead, too. Bob's funeral will be tomorrow. Dick shook his hand without being able to say anything. Tears came from his eyes as if squeezed out by his handshake. In the full sunlight of the window Raeburn feels his knee itch and his arms itch where the blisters have shrunk to small sores. The back of his neck itches at the shirt collar like a child forced to dress for church. At First Baptist, Mary Ann had been good, repeating only once her "We killed her like we made her," when Larry Gray gave his sermon, as if in church she sensed it was obscene.

Someone refills Raeburn's glass with more of the whiskey he hasn't wanted earlier. He knows he can name this person he thanks, if he has to. He holds the glass two handed, like Al did his hat. It was only out at the cemetery that Mary Ann lost control. Now she's fine, in the kitchen with other women. Not fine, he doesn't mean that. He's ashamed to have thought that. She's more in control of herself, is what he means. He wonders if he's supposed to be in the kitchen. Should he be doing the rounds? Are these people his guests, is he supposed, for heaven's sake, to be *hosting* his daughter's funeral? The talking in low voices comes to him as a buzz. At least the church was quiet. Larry Gray's voice was quiet, gray, what they call white noise. Only from time to time it was rent by one of Kate's girlfriends screaming "No!" and weeping behind him.

Someone is asking if he needs anything. He knows the man is unaware of the question's irony. As he shakes his head, he feels the man's arm come awkwardly onto his shoulder and move quickly off. He can name him, too. It's Pete Bruelich, who's put himself in charge of drinks. He meant did he need anything to drink. Raeburn sips from the whiskey and Pete, relieved, goes looking for drinkers with empties. Raeburn thinks there are few men in the kitchen, if any. The men out here aren't talking much. They want something to do, like Pete, like Al Jarowski out parking cars. Not that the men haven't compassion. It's that they have no practice talking about it or touching each other. If he announced he needed them to put up a frame for a new house, they'd start at once, relieved. You could also drive nails or mortise a corner cut with tenderness. Kate's friends are all over the place—back yard, upstairs. They wear dark glasses and frown so much when they speak to him that their foreheads look bruised. A hand is rubbing his hand.

Eleanor's hand. He walks away from the window with Eleanor. He says, "How is she?" He can smell the *picadilo* from the kitchen.

"Not good. I'm very worried about her. And you, Willy. God damn."

Her face is saggier than ever. The flesh of her cheeks hangs in a series of teardrops. He says, "I'm finding it hard to focus." She says, "I know, but it's Mary Ann who's taking this so terribly."

He feels angry. Does Eleanor expect Mary Ann to take this well? He watches his glass fill up with whiskey again, like in some fairy tale for drunks. He wonders if in the kitchen Mary Ann can be saying that terrible thing she says to him. He says, "Why, what is she saying?" Eleanor says, "Nothing at all. That's what I mean."

He gets the point. Mary Ann saying nothing is bad because she's a woman. Him saying nothing is good, though this is bad because that's how men are. Eleanor says, "I'll tell Mary Ann you're okay." He nods. Mary Ann will really like to hear that he's okay. He heads to the front door because he wants to go to the back yard but not through the kitchen. People make a respectful space for him to get by.

It's hot out back in the sun. The steamy air has a chemical smell like at the dry cleaners. His dark suit is hot and mothballed. He touches the yellow alamandas whose plastic perfection Kate also doesn't like. Didn't. If they're somewhere awful where they can't speak, he says, "Pretty as a yellow alamanda," and Kate smiles. Smiled. The back yard is full of shy kids standing still like sad rabbits. Raeburn goes to the back under the Spanish lime. He kicks at the earth by its trunk.

There was a small bit of earth at his toe by the open grave. Red earth on the fake grass carpet. He held Mary Ann's arm and looked at the tip of his black shined shoe. That was when she started her "We killed her like we made her." Worse, she said, as loud as Larry Gray's intoning, "Fucking in the boat when we should have been going to find Kate." He said, "No, sweetheart," but she went on repeating "We killed her like we made her," over and over, a mantra of misery against Larry's "belief in the resurrection and the life everlasting in Jesus Christ our Lord, Amen." Her mantra of truth.

He drains the glass and looks up into the tree and sees the planks of Kate's old tree house. He sets down the glass and moves around to the climbing spikes. The tree has grown over them so they're little more than head studs. He stretches his hands to two, lifts a leg and climbs hand over hand. At the limbs, he pulls up until he's under the planks and pulls himself through. Mickey Berman is sitting on a corner of the platform with his arms wrapped around his knees.

Mickey says, "I saw it and had to come up."

Raeburn nods. The two of them had built the treehouse for Kate when she was ten.

They sit without being able to say anything.

Finally, Raeburn says, "I should have taught her baseball."

Mickey says, "I should have taught her piano."

Raeburn can see down to cars still coming in from Pine Avenue and Al directing other cars out. He can see most of Pine Shores. Even with twenty years of fast growth trees, the streets still show strictly parallel between the curve of the outer avenue like the strings of a heavy harp.

He shuts his eyes and sees himself out on his boat the night he planned to kill himself. Up behind Coastal's survey boat he's tipping out drums of gasoline onto the oil slick at its stern. He fires his flare gun into the water and the gasoline bursts into a line of fireworks that sizzles in a fuse back to the ship where Roy leans over the stern to see the ragged orange arms of flame engulf him....

Raeburn opens his eyes. He thinks of all the flowers down there for Kate. Roy and Anita Higgs have sent twelve dozen red roses. Probably Roy's idea, so many: a gross of roses. Of course, neither of them has shown up.

He looks across at the second floor windows. At their bedroom where last night Mary Ann lay open eyed until he left and went downstairs. He tiptoed back to see if Mary Ann was at last asleep. He knew not to touch her. His touch brought on her *rigor mortis*. It snapped open her eyes. Mary Ann and Kate.

He looks through the leaves over at Kate's bedroom and sees as on the night he surprised them, Kate and Bob naked, her legs wrapped around him. Of course not, it's some damned kids on her bed. He's ashamed to ask Mickey if he sees this; he pushes off the planks, twists through the hole, drops among branches and slides fast down the trunk. He rushes across the yard and in the kitchen door. The women turn around, look up, and stop talking. They talk to him, they touch his arm. He says he's fine, thanks, thanks, he's all right. Mary Ann turns from the sink and takes his arm. He feels great love and sorrow and bends to kiss her cheek. She says, "You've torn your jacket sleeve." He pulls back and goes into the hall. He wants to stop the kids up in Kate's room but Mary Ann's old aunt Louise is coming down the stairs one at a time on her cane. She says, "Dear Bill" and as he twists past, "Yes, it's free now."

Up on the landing, he sees Eleanor's son Steve with a girl near Kate's open door. Steve says, "Hi, Uncle Bill." Raeburn says, "What in hell do you think you're doing in there?" The girl says, "I'm Georgia Thomas, Mr. Raeburn, Kate's friend." He glares at her. She says, "I put some flowers in her room. I..." She weeps and Steve puts his arms around her. Raeburn looks in. The bed is neatly made, untouched. There is a vase of waxy white roses by the bed. He says, "I'm sorry. I was confused." He pats the girl's shaking shoulders. He feels he needs a haircut, feels his hair growing as he stands looking into his nephew's bloodshot eyes. He goes downstairs. Charlie Styles is waiting to shake his hand. Charlie says, "My heart and Barbara's go out to you. She's in with Mary Ann." Raeburn says, "Why do you think this is turning out so women-only and men-only?" Charlie Styles looks confused. He says, "Bill, in addition to that line of credit from Mickey Berman at the bank, if you need extra, if there are additional expenses, you have credit with us. Lowest terms, nothing to do with Roy, you understand."

Raeburn understands. A banker condoling. Like the girl's white roses or Linda Martinez's *picadilo* in the kitchen. If he had a Mafia friend, the man would now offer him a contract *gratis*. He says, "Good of you, Charlie. Have a drink." People come up to him. He knows them all. There are flowers from the Dean of Freshmen at Miami. All that tuition money saved, he thinks. Bankers throwing money at him now. They are doing well. They should have thought of killing Kate before. Ritchie Martinez is hugging him, crying over his shoulder a little drunk. He pats Ritchie's back and moves off. Pete Bruelich puts another glass of whiskey in his hands. Pete is doing a good bartending job. Raeburn says, "Hold this, Pete. I'm just stepping out for fresh air."

Raeburn closes the front door and shakes hands with new-comers as he moves along the path. It is lined with funeral flowers in cellophane. The flowers go right out and along both sides of the picket fence out front. Many bouquets and wreaths are pink, as if they had just had a baby girl. They still could have. Mary Ann still has periods. But they will not. Even if they pass their egg and sperm tests top of the class, they are not going to try. Mary Ann lies rigid, mortified.

Al Jarowski sees him getting into his blocked-in pickup and begins backing cars out, double and triple parking to make space. He nods to Al as he passes. Someone will tell Al off for letting him go. Probably Eleanor. He drives slowly past Flying Fish and Galleon Drive, Hibiscus and Jacaranda Drive, the streets of Kate's alphabet. Old Roy's streets and everyone believed in the streets and in the houses and in the bright kitchens and in the daughters. Soon he finds himself before the old Higgs Construction Offices on De Leon. Roy Jr. has sentimentally kept them on. He parks at the side and takes out the gun in its oilskin from the glove compartment. He has taken this out of the house to protect Mary Ann from herself.

He walks up the stairs: tongue-in-groove walls, photos of the early projects. At the door he tucks in the strips of fabric hanging from his sleeve. He doesn't himself know why. The secretaries look up when he walks in. They look quickly among themselves. He asks for Roy and they all say how sorry they are for him. He thanks them and again asks for Roy. One of them says she thinks he's in Tallahassee. Another says she thinks by now he'll be in Baton Rouge. He nods and walks through to the inner corridor and down to Roy's office. He feels the weight of the gun in his pocket as he opens the door. Nobody's there. This was Old Roy's office. Maybe if he'd grown up and stopped using Higgs' father and son as fathers, he would have learned to be a father himself. To take care of his daughter. And wife. He leaves the office and walks back down the corridor. He sees the secretaries think he's a little soft in the head with grief. They say again how sorry they are. He knows their names. He thanks them. He feels that his hair is on fire. Going downstairs he remembers as a boy trailing his fingers over the tongue-in-groove when he came here with his father.

In the pickup, he rewraps the pistol in the oilskin and puts it back into the glove compartment. He considers going out to the nursing home and shooting his father. But the father he wants to shoot died all those years ago before the playoff. He turns north on De Leon and drives slowly out of town. He passes the bridge to Groves Island. Roy isn't there. Roy is gone. He remembers

Larry Gray say "life everlasting." If you believe in life after death, you'll believe anything. He believes in death after death. He turns west into the old quarry road and, quarter of a mile down, swerves past the concrete blocking slabs onto the side path the kids have cut to squeeze their hotrods through. In here the road is cracked. Flat cap rock shows through. It's not as he remembers it. Black and red mangroves have walked inland and covered the old mudflats from the shore to the roadside hammock. He pulls onto a slab of cap rock, stops and gets out. He smells the salt and mangrove bitterness. Green, impenetrable, guilty. About his mother. But about *what?*

He walks along the old road sighting on a higher clump of trees in the hammock. His arm throbs where the tree spikes scraped. He's hot and itchy in his dark suit and his shirt and his tie. It is the day of his daughter's funeral. The day of his wife's funeral. Abreast of the taller trees he strikes into the mangroves. He shields his eyes with his arm and pushes ahead through the whip and tangle. When he breaks through, he's looking into the red of a grove of gumbo-limbo trees beside the old path. He puts his head against a big trunk and pulls off papery strips of red bark. He looks through them. They're the color of Kate's hair. Now he moves fast along the path. He twists around buttonwood and cabbage palm and gumbo-limbo. He stops and listens to the screaming of black-headed gulls. It is off here that it happened. He caught his father beating his mother. Not hitting her, twisting her arm. There was a sound, a screaming. He moves faster. Trees, branches, sinkholes underfoot. He moves out of the hammock and makes his way through the scrub mangrove towards the water. Dark blue strips of cloth flap off both his jacket arms. He concentrates on staying on the cap rock, here pocked with sinkholes. He gives it up and jogs on the brown-orange mud. It sucks at his shoes until he stands on the four-foot beach strip, panting.

Raeburn pulls off his shoes and socks and rolls his trousers up and walks into the shallows. He knows he's never had much dress sense. Mary Ann used to say he looked best without any clothes. He stops to feel a small breeze. The water laps at his knees, just below his trousers. He sits down in the water. It's midway up his chest. The dark blue dress tie bobs on the water. What is he doing here? He stands up and looks along the shoreline and sees the lagoon and edge of the stilt platform.

It takes him some time to work his way along the shore and around. He doesn't want to do this. He has to. Around the shack door hang small bits of bright-colored cloth. Stars and crescent moons cut from tin are tacked up. Some are shiny; most are rust orange and have stained the wood in reddish rivulets. When the wind blows, small ticking and clacking sounds come from the metal and the rags stick out like tongues.

Raeburn knocks on the door. He waits. He knocks again, heavier. If no one answers he can leave. There is no answer. He opens the door. Caloosahatchie Joe is lying curled on his side on an iron bed. His eyes and mouth are wide open. He may be dead. He says, "Cal Joe?"

The head jerks, says, "Huh? What? Who's that there?"

He says, "Don't you know without knowing? Aren't you the seventh son of a seventh son? Don't you have six senses?"

Cal Joe heaves his legs over the bed, pushes up slowly and stretches his arms. "I don't know. Damn, I don't have five good senses left, lest six. Who are you?"

As Cal Joe rises, the room expands outwards and upwards and settles down again. Cal Joe has a yellow bandana tied tight over his skull. He's wearing a pink sweatshirt and blue cut-offs. His legs are sheened with scars. He shuffles out without looking at Raeburn. Raeburn hears him walking around the deck. He hears him peeing. He hears yawns, groans, and stomping. Finally, footsteps back, and the door opens.

"Sweet Jesus, it's Bill Raeburn."

In the open door, Cal Joe's silhouette is a foot taller. Magic tricks. Raeburn's hands rise against a memory: a shadow he has to duck from and close his eyes. He feels hands on his shoulders.

"I am truly sorry for your loss. I didn't make you out. Sit down here in the chair."

He takes off his wet jacket and puts it on the back of the chair and sits down.

Cal Joe says, "Lord God, you lose your lovely girl."

He loosens his tie and unbuttons his collar. He smells his own reek and something delicate and sharp from the shack, like vanilla and ginger. "Would you have something I could eat? Bread or crackers?"

"Crackers, yes. Happen a great-grandchild of mine came by yesterday and her mother brought lots."

Raeburn takes the box. "Thank you. It's Hendry, isn't it. Joseph Hendry."

"That's it, like the county up north of Big Cypress."

Raeburn holds a box of animal crackers. It has a flat string handle and is designed with animal cages on a circus train. He opens it carefully, as he did when he was a child, as he's taught Kate. He looks close and eats an elephant. Then maybe a buffalo; the crackers are always so lumpish and indistinguishable. Sweet, bland. Cal Joe hands him a tin mug. "I'm sorry that I stink so."

"That's okay. You're sorrowful. Poison's got to come out."

He eats more of the innocents and lets the coffee flood over them. It makes a mush in his mouth that he swallows with more of the sweet, chicory coffee. He has to get on with it. "You know something about me, Joe."

"What you mean?" Cal Joe's face is full of smooth marks, like sinkholes in the cap rock.

"A few weeks ago when I brought Mickey here in my boat you said you were waiting for me. Mickey said you told him I had to see you."

"That wasn't nothin. That was puttin on a show for Mickey. He spects that."

Raeburn feels he's drying to the chair. Tiny bridges of salt are crystallizing between his shirt and trousers and the wood. "No. You know something about me out here when I was sixteen, the day before the playoff. Me and my father and mother. Please tell me."

"I don't know nothin about what you're sayin."

Raeburn finishes the box. His mouth is mealy. On the shelf by the sink are six more boxes of animal crackers. Kate had never wanted to eat them, only to play with them. Raeburn stands and goes to the shelf. "That morning with Mickey, you called me 'hero.' I haven't been a hero since the playoff game when I was sixteen. Since the day before when I was out here with my father and mother. You were there, I know. What did you see?"

"I didn't see nothin. And it don't mean anythin, me callin you 'hero.' I also call you Jason. Jason and his Argue-not, wasn't it? That was to give Mickey a kick. I get a kick out of it, too, but it don't mean nothin."

Next to the crackers is a brown Barbie doll in a pink tutu. It looks like voodoo to Raeburn. "That day out here, I caught my father beating up my mother out on the flats. I went crazy. I beat him badly, I remember. But I can't remember what happened then. Something did. Next day he had that accident. He knew better. He was tryin to kill himself. He did the next closest thing, sitting mindless in the nursing home all these years. And then my mother just shriveling up and dying soon after. Something in me did, too. And my life's stopped again with Kate's death and I have to know. You know. I know you know."

Cal Joe shakes his yellow-bandanaed head. "Man, it's just your girl's dyin make you suppose there was more bad stuff all that time ago."

Raeburn goes to the bed. "Don't voodoo me."

"I ain't. Maybe you better get on outa here." The yellow head keeps shaking.

Raeburn's hand shoots under Cal Joe's jaw and pushes his head back. He can feel the bristles of hair along the web of his hand. "I've dreamed of a shadow out there. Something jumping up. I know it was you." He pushes Cal Joe's head further back. His eyes close in pain.

"Time was, even you couldn't have got hold on me like this. Still, I can look after myself, for an old man."

Raeburn feels a scratch on his pants at his scrotum. He looks down to see the point of an eight-inch kitchen knife at the bottom of his fly.

"If this cut you here, your pride gonna hurt. I go up some, this goin into your liver and there's no fixin it."

Raeburn keeps looking at the knife. His left hand flashes across Cal Joe's hand and the knife flies off.

"Damn! Damn!" yells Cal Joe. "You hurt my hand, man!"

He tips back Cal Joe's head until the thick folds of his neck are stretched into pale lines.

"Tell me."

He feels the nod and lets go. Cal Joe coughs and sucks air and rubs his throat. "You a mean, hard man, Bill. You better be, you hear what you makin me tell."

Raeburn brings his chair up and sits facing Cal Joe. "Tell me now."

Cal Joe says, "You right, I was there. Out near the flats I see two folks, your folks, out there too far off to make out. I was checkin things out cause I used to grow stuff out of big cans them days. Tomato, pepper, okra, like that. Also I had a cash crop of some marijuana, so I needed to know there wasn't trouble comin. So I got around the other side to check them out and by then it's the three of you and I can make you out. You and Bob shoutin and your momma squattin off to one side, quiet like. Then I see

135

you beat him up, like you say. Then your momma she gets up and starts tryin to pull you off him, and she's huggin at you to try to hold you back. So I figure it ain't concernin my crops."

"That's what Mickey saw."

"Mickey? I didn't see Mickey."

"Then?"

"Yeah, then. Well, just as I'm goin off, I see you start twistin your momma's arm."

"Maybe I was holding her."

"No, sir. You was hurtin her bad, bendin her arm around. Hey, I don't have to go on."

"Go on."

"Well you twist her right down to the ground, and all this time she makin—I forgot to say this—she was makin the same sound I was hearing earlier, thought it was some red-shoulder hawk callin. Not a sound a person ought to make, a bad sound. Then I see you take off runnin, and your momma she got up and went to where your poppa was lyin and she started to tend to him. Then I took off. I wasn't mixin with no family fight, specially no goddamn white family. So I got back to my farmin area, and a few minutes later you come and run almost right over me, you runnin so crazy, and I got scared and stood up and waved you off my crop like I was a scarecrow, and you took a look at me and jump and turned back runnin across the flats looked like twice as fast. I won't never forget how crazy you looked. By the time I figured it, you was gone. All these years I thought if you forget about it, I don't blame you. But I wasn't going to tell you. I wasn't going lookin for trouble."

Raeburn hears the water lap under the shack. He says, "Thank you." He puts on his stinking jacket and leaves. He closes the door and takes out his wallet and draws out all his wet money. He pulls the bills apart. One hundred and forty eight dollars. One Four Eight. Adds to thirteen, if he wanted voodoo. There is no

voodoo. What there is is worse. He loosens two thumbtacks. One
Four Eight is a bargain for such knowledge. He leaves the money
drying among the bits of rag, tin moons, and rusted stars. He
walks down the planking in the salt stink of himself.

Now he knows it all. When his mother held him, begging him
to stop beating his father, he first tried to get her away, take her
home. When she wouldn't go and said her place was with her husband, he'd understood, even at sixteen, that she in some way liked
the beatings his father gave her, or, at least, had chosen that high
bird screaming silence of her pain. A bride of pain. His father had
never punched her; he'd hurt her in a way that wouldn't show by
twisting her arm. So all he at sixteen could do was show her he was
as good a man as his father. More twisted. He'd twisted her more.
He sees that all his life his strength has been directed against the
wrong people: father, mother, daughter, and wife. Now he knows.
He begins running to his pickup through the mangroves.

Chapter Ten _____

MAYBE I SHOULD HAVE STAYED in Turtle Key. Hindsight. I didn't stay. Bill had vanished on the day of Kate's funeral. In the late afternoon, he'd drawn out in cash the credit line I'd set up for him and Mary Ann, all thirty thousand dollars. The bank called me the next morning, and I said, "That's all right," as if this were perfectly within my expectations. All I could figure was whatever Bill was doing, he was planning on being away for some time. I didn't tell Mary Ann; I wouldn't have even if she were able to take it in. But she'd gone away, too, somewhere way beyond shock and mourning. I told Eleanor. I might have guessed her response.

She said, "Get your ass out of here and find him. The money you gave him probably gave him the idea to take off."

I gave her a look. It must have sunk in, because she said, "I know the money was for their debts. But it isn't easy coping with Mary Ann."

Maybe I should have gone looking for Bill or done anything but join Anita and Roy. It's all hindsight. With Bill gone, there seemed no point in my staying. I wanted to leave all the TK mess behind—Bill, Mary Ann, Kate's death, the oil spill, and the mess I'd made with Charlene—and just unwind and enjoy myself. The funny thing was, from the moment I got to the airport, I knew my enjoyment wouldn't include an affair with Anita. No affair, no romance, no flirtation. What I wanted, I decided between touching down at Cancun and taking off for Mérida, was a vacation from flirtation and its messy aftermaths.

The chance to tell Anita came immediately. The hotel desk clerk told me she was out at the pool. I had them take the luggage to my room and went outside via the bar, where I picked up a tequila as a token of my holiday spirit, as well as for some courage. She was on her own, in a white silk bathrobe, on a chaise back from the pool. She was reading a book, so she didn't see me until my shadow stopped across her. The book was *Evelina*: pretty esoteric for me. I wondered if I was meant to be impressed. She brought the book down and looked at me through her checked sunglasses. Then she pulled them down her nose and looked at me and put out her arms. Her gray eyes stayed still. I took her hand and kissed it and said, "It's nice to be here."

"And me? Is it nice to see me?"

"It is. It's very nice to see you."

"Are you angry, after all, that I didn't come down for the funeral?"

"No."

"But?"

"But let's just be friends, Anita, just friends, and have a good time."

She pushed her glasses back up her nose. "Of course. We'll have a nice time. Roy's up in the room working."

She was offended but didn't intend to show it. That suited me more than if she'd challenged my change of heart. I think, as things turned out, I paid for this. I know Bill did.

We had a good time, those three days in Mérida. Certainly we spoke of Kate and Bob Davis's deaths, of Mary Ann's breakdown and Bill's disappearance (they didn't seem to know about his taking the money, and I didn't volunteer to tell them), but we didn't dwell on it. Roy appeared genuinely ashamed of the way he'd believed in the infallibility of Coastal's engineering. He also seemed genuinely pleased to see me. I supposed he sensed the different feeling between Anita and me. At any rate, they were good company. She knew Mexican and Indian history, and Roy, with no need to play the bubba, was bright and funny, and something of a scholar on hummingbirds, some examples of which could usually be found hanging around the garden out by the swimming pool. The evening before we were to set off for the Mayan ruins at Uxmal, Roy said he'd had a call and had to get back to Tallahassee to work with (or did he say over?) an environmental committee investigating the spill. He thought he could join us down there in two days. I thought it could be a test of my no-flirting decision.

I passed, as they say, in thought and deed. On the drive from Mérida to Uxmal, Anita and I actually talked. She told me how she wrote these occasional travel articles for newspapers and magazines, but she wanted to write short stories. She'd taken a workshop or two in Washington, but she didn't have the time to hang in there. I think I told her the tale of me and New York City and my nose-candy answer to my piano problem.

We checked into our hotel, a big old hacienda building around tropical gardens. In the afternoon we met and drove into the ruins. They struck me as very melancholy relics. I couldn't help thinking of all those gold and jewel clad priests in a top-heavy culture. In the evening, we talked about the day's sights and planned the next day's visit. We set out, next morning, for the ruins of a phallic temple. After walking an hour in the heat, Anita sat down on a boulder and wondered if maybe we'd taken the wrong path. I looked at the boulder and said it was the right path: she was sitting on a huge stone penis. I found this funny, but not sexy, so I felt sure I wasn't going to flirt.

What happened was stranger, though it didn't involve Anita or any sexual experience. In the late afternoon, I went back to the ruins on my own. Anita was swimming. There wasn't time left until dark for me to get very far, just into the open plaza before Uxmal's most famous building, the Pyramid of the Magician. I am not, as I've said before, much of a jock. And I was still tired from our morning's trek. But looking up, I decided to climb the huge building. The steps were high, a foot and a half high, each one, and the tread was narrow. I went up holding a safety chain strung from iron rods. Coming down the other side of the chain was a file of tourists, tall, blond men and women, all in floppy cloth sun hats with appliqué daffodils. Swedish, I decided. My legs ached, but after a while I saw I was alone up there, and it gave me the energy to go on to the topmost temple. I sat back against it and rested.

Above me, the sky was filled with small white clouds, regular and flat to the horizon. The huge, ruined city was ringed with dark forest. After a while, I stood. I was filled with an emotion that was neither elation nor despair but contained both. I wasn't thinking of myself or of any particular thing. Maybe it was the grandeur and decay of the place, maybe I remembered I was standing where priests ripped the hearts from human sacrifices and held them up, still beating, to the sun. I didn't want to go back down holding the safety chain, like the sensible Swedes. I thought of the old song "Frenesi." Frenzy, fiesta time in Mexico.

I looked down: it was so steep the steps didn't show. It looked like an upended avenue. I went away from the chain side, to the middle. The Swedes were huddled on the ground looking up. I thought I'd try a few steps and if it was scary, I'd move back to the chain. I balanced backwards and took a steep step down. And then another, jigging my hip up to half jump. It was definitely scary, but my legs were too weak to hold me back. I could either sit down fast and scrape my pride for a step or two and stop, or let it happen. Then I thought, "Frenesi" and let go. I was going down fast, faster. I was high stepping, flying down the bloodied steps to the lyrics of the song: *"It was fiesta time in Mexico, and so I stopped a while to see the show—"*

By then I couldn't have stopped without falling a hundred or more feet. I couldn't see the steps. My thighs were shaking at each jump impact so I leaned forward to force them. I was thinking Frenesi, Frenzy, running down with my arms flapping to keep from falling or to fly down to the crowd at the bottom. Fiesta, fiesta, faster and faster down and down in Mexico, I couldn't stop, my heart was still up at the high altar, the people were cheering and the ground rushed up to meet me.

They were actually applauding. I found myself standing in a grove of Swedes who shouted Olé!

I felt incredibly happy. Never before or after have I felt like that. It wasn't just a physical triumph (I was frightened to think of it); it was as if I'd left my body, or for a few seconds had inhabited the body of another animal. More to the point, it was the moment that sealed my affair with Anita. As sure as if she'd been at the top and we'd made love up there. Not that it entered my mind then.

A day later, a call came from Roy saying he was held up but would meet us in Belize City in three days, from where our expedition into the Guatemalan rain forest would begin. And even then, on our own, going back to Mérida and fixing up the chartered plane, I didn't give Anita anything but friends-only thoughts.

We got to Belize City in the morning. Roy was due in about eleven that night. We put up in the best hotel in town, which isn't saying much. I've been in some crummy places, in and out of the

States, but Belize City takes the crumb cake. Anita just lay around and read that day. I went walking and taxiing around trying to find at least something I liked. I couldn't. We decided to meet at the hotel bar, have dinner in the restaurant and wait for Roy.

After I showered, I stood looking out my window. I saw only palms and clipped grass, an avenue and then the turquoise sea. I could have been anywhere. I remembered Ginny Gordon saying as much in Turtle Key. I could have been in one of a hundred places in west Florida. Except for the boats. They were the problem. They were mostly dull wood hulls with squat, gaffed sails, and the sails were mostly patchwork. They were coming from or working down to Haulover Creek. And if I looked even slightly left or right, I'd see the waterfront and know I wasn't anywhere but the best part of some place pathetic. I went over to the desk, where I'd unfolded my practice keyboard, a plastic dummy I use to keep my fingers in shape. But I was too nervous to practice. I felt I was running around the world in order to stay still. I knew there was another life. I'd felt it sometimes at the piano; I'd felt it flying down the Pyramid of the Magician.

Ten minutes later, I was down at the bar when Anita came in. She was wearing a little, white cotton dress, sleeveless with white straps. It was phenomenal and she knew it. She said, "I thought I'd wear a real dress. This is the last chance I'll have before weeks of bush shorts and trousers."

"It's very pretty. What will you drink?"

"What's that, rum punch?"

"Yes."

"I'll have that. Would you mind, awfully, if we found some place to eat that isn't this hotel?"

"I don't much like it, either. We'll drink to going out for dinner." Out beyond the hotel lawn, a splintery boat was lowering its rag sail. Suddenly, it looked romantic.

We walked out from the hotel to Fort George and watched

the sunlight go slant and dark yellow over the water. Out past the mangrove keys, the clouds appeared like lines of highlighter. I found myself telling Anita about running down the Pyramid at Uxmal, and what I thought it meant to me. Until then, I'd wanted to keep it to myself.

She listened and was quiet for some time. She said, "Sometimes it seems our lives have everything but life."

I tried not to hear this as banal. I suggested we find a bar with local music. There was plenty of time for dinner. We walked the wide, looping street back towards town. We passed some nice enough government buildings, but even here the underlying smell was mud, like a reminder that any half good hurricane could drive the town back into the swamp it rose from. We came out onto a busy cross street. Down the block, a crowd of young men hung around the swing bridge over Haulover Creek. The air was wet and heavy. I could chew it; it tasted like grains of mud. Anita went silky with sweat: neck, shoulders, breasts. As we came towards the bridge, young men called out. "Uh-uh-uh, baby!" "*Ai-ai, qué huapa!* "You comin heeya, girl, you wan somtin good!" As if I wasn't there.

"Should we go back?"

She said, "I like it here."

The bridge, too, was crowded with young men. The light was strange, as if the heart of Belize City were lit by low watt bulbs, like in a hot refrigerator. We looked back up the creek where the water was barely visible, it was so boat choked, hull along hull and crisscross of mast sticks, like a logjam a mile long. We were leaning over the bridge. Anita's short, tight white dress and blond hair were attracting too much attention. Young men strolled by and called at her. "Pretty, pretty baby." "*Qué titas lindas.* "She wanna suck my dick, I ain't sayin no." "You all right?"

A voice repeated right behind me, "You all right?" with a slight English accent.

I turned and said, "Yes, thanks."

The man, a Creole, said, "No, 'you all right' means hello, here. You need a taxi, there's my taxi. I wouldn't walk around, you and the lady, the other side of the bridge. Very insalubrious."

I asked him if he knew a place with good music. "No, problem," he said. Twice on the thirty-yard walk to his cab, someone came up and asked, "Need anything for your night out?" Each time, the cab driver said, "Get off it."

We got in and drove slowly off the bridge. He turned and said, "They were trying to sell you drugs." He blew his horn to move the people in the street. He turned and said, "All gangs now. Crips and Bloods, they copycat L.A. The town's never been so bad. Used to be a little local grass, like that. Now it's imported gangs, imported drugs."

I noticed that our protective cabdriver was taking us straight into the insalubrious side of the city. I felt it couldn't be worse than the salubrious. He turned and said, "Club doesn't look much, but there's a good group in from Livingston." I'd heard a group from Livingston. I told Anita it was an English-speaking town on the Caribbean, in Guatemala, just south of Belize. It was full of good musicians playing a mix of Creole, salsa, and Jamaican music. She said she was impressed. I said that was the sum of my Guatemalan knowledge. We turned into a very narrow street and suddenly the cab was surrounded by a gang of young boys banging on the roof and doors and fenders. The driver turned and said, "Don't do nothing, sir. Wait." He reached down beside him, rolled down his window, and threw a handful of small change out into the street. The boys fell away and the cab picked up speed. I found my heart was pounding. Anita was laughing. She said, "Isn't this better than that suffocating hotel?" We turned another corner and stopped by a single story concrete building. Its one small window showed a blue neon sign: Lord's Bar. The driver turned and said, "Here you are. You could set a time and I'd be back to pick you up, save you walking through all that." I started to agree, but then I thought I could be as cool as Anita, especially after telling her the story of my magic at Uxmal. I said, "No, that's okay," and paid him.

Lord's bar inside was a pleasant surprise. Cool air conditioning. Smoothed concrete walls painted in tans and shades of red. Black lacquer chairs and tables, a bandstand, and a long back-mirrored bar that wouldn't look out of place in Rockefeller Plaza. "Nice," Anita said. I said, "Nice. Drug money." The place was empty except for a couple at the bar. We went and sat a few seats away and ordered rum punch. The drinks came in large bowl glasses. Perfect rum punch, peppered with fresh nutmeg and light to taste but strong. We toasted our coming trip, drank and went silent. We were looking in the mirror at the other couple. They were very fine looking and elegant, a black couple sitting to Anita's side. I saw the man glance at Anita's legs. Her dress sat high on her crossed thighs. We ordered more rum punch. Anita leaned into me and whispered, "See the four of us in the mirror? They have darker skins, but we look more African." I looked in the mirror. In a way she was right: her heavy lips and long almond eyes, and I thought I might pass for a pale Ethiopian. The man kept glancing at Anita. I was sure he could see her pants. I wondered if she knew that. When the drinks came, Anita toasted: "To the four of us," and laughed.

The bartender put on a CD. Latin piano. Anita put her hand on my wrist: "Let me guess. Joe Loco?" I said, "Yes. Now I'm impressed." She said, "I know lots of things, if you got to know me." We talked about Afro-Cuban music. She told me how once, at a club, she'd asked Machito's trumpeter Chocolato to have a drink at her table and had described the orchestra's sound as "curtains of brass," and Chocolato had liked that. I told her I liked it too. I asked the bartender what time the band was coming on. "Oh, maybe ten or eleven. Eleven-thirty for sure." We had another rum punch to toast this group from Livingston we were going to miss, and then we left.

It was hot and wet outside. She said, "We're going to walk around and find a place to eat here." I said, "We're going to walk around insalubriously and do that."

We started walking. I said I'd better hold her hand so the men would know she was with someone. We held hands. Two young men went by. One said in Spanish how very well he would fuck this blond.

Anita smiled. I said, "Would you smile if this were Washington?"

"I wouldn't be in this part of Washington. But here, tonight, it's sexy. Don't you think?"

I said, "Sure."

We turned a corner. A young couple was kissing in a doorway. "Very sweet," I said. Anita said, "Just darling."

We walked down dark, crowded streets, down empty narrow streets with dim lights. The air thickened with insects. We didn't ask directions for a restaurant. We came to a canal and crossed a bridge into a part of town all wooden. There were houses on stilts, tilted storefronts, low light and deep shadow. There was laughter off front porches, there were smells of pepper and curry, sharp piss smells from the gutters, and the soft smell of chocolate. We walked on gang streets with customized American lowriders as long as the houses were wide. I knew it was a little crazy to be doing this, but I was sure we'd find a good place to eat. We were drunk. We passed whorehouses, three in a row brightly lit. Reggae poured over the streets, the bass throbbing so heavy that the wooden walls jumped. No one hassled us. It was as if our drunkenness protected us. A fat, olive skinned woman leaned over a banister and asked if we needed a room for the night? For an hour? No? She herself would join us. No? Anita and I laughed and looked at each other and looked away. Anita's dress had risen almost to her buttocks. She must have known. We passed a house with a big party going on, *cumbia* music jumping out. We could see in the windows the half undressed women dancing with men and dancing with other women. I thought Anita was enjoying imagining herself a whore in these houses.

We saw the bright sign across a canal: UNCLE's, on a big, tilted wooden house. We said at the same time, "See, we knew we'd find it." We walked along and crossed the bridge. Oil and mud smells rose up from the canal. Shouting and laughter down from the dark, moored boats.

Inside, the restaurant was brilliant with fluorescent light. The tables were covered in white paper. We found one at a wall near a flight of stairs. People were drinking beer and rum and eating fish. It smelled good. A young girl came and we ordered grilled shrimp and glasses of white rum. We drank waiting for the shrimp. On the wall above the table were old photos of men posed with various big fish. The colors had turned so that all the fish were baby blue and all the men were yellow with green spots. We laughed. I couldn't take my eyes off Anita. When the shrimp came we ordered more rum, and I went upstairs to the men's room. When I came out, I stopped at the top landing and looked down at Anita. She'd worked herself part out of her dress on that chair: its skirt to the top of her thighs, its top down so that her breasts were half bared. I sat down seeing the fine sweat over her lips and on her shoulders. We ate shrimp and drank white rum. I had no more chat. I said, "I'm going upstairs again. Go up after I do." I went up without waiting to see her expression. She would or she wouldn't.

Upstairs, I opened a door between the men's and ladies'. It was a storage closet. The hallway smelled of wet wood and fried fish. I knocked on the ladies' door. No answer. I went in. A basin, a mirror, two empty stalls, a floor of dirty linoleum. I heard footsteps outside. If it was someone else I'd say sorry and go. I stepped out of my shoes and took off my pants and underpants. Anita came in and laughed to see me like that and shut the door. I pulled her dress over her head and pulled down her pants. I heard the knock of her shoes kicked off as we pulled each other to the floor. I entered her while I held the hem of her dress bunched in my fist so that it pulled tight to her face. She was already moving under me, her legs around me, laughing, moaning so that I was moaning with her and half laughing in the ecstatic craziness of it, with the two of us making so much noise and anyone able to walk in on us fucking and get us arrested for fucking or join us fucking on the dirty floor, crazy in the smell of the mud and linoleum and wet wood and fish. Anita pulled me into her so hard it was as if I were through her as we came, she screaming so loud that even under the gag of her dress I had to press it bunched over her mouth while I moaned and gasped my pleasure. Then she pulled at my arm and pulled the dress off her face and bit my neck hard. She was panting. She said, "That's it, you fucking bastard, you did that. I love you. I'll fuck you forever." It seemed possible right then that we could live a life consisting entirely of fucking on public toilet floors. Then we washed and dressed at the basin and mirror, looking at each other, kissing at the mirror as if it was in our own bathroom. Going down, we passed a woman coming up the stairs and said good evening.

We had the restaurant call us a cab. We drove through the streets in a quiet delirium of slowly receding thrills, like the tide going out that can still move up the beach to make you wet.

We got back in time to go to our rooms and change, meet again and agree that if we were asked, our story would be exactly what occurred, except in its one particular. We'd finished coffee in a sitting alcove off the lobby, when Roy arrived. A big, burly man was with him. Roy hugged Anita, shook hands with me and then glanced back at Anita. "So you're all right?" he said neither to me nor to her. He could as well have said, "So you've become lovers," so clear was it that he knew. Then he introduced the man with him as George Hapwood, an associate. He suggested we all go to the bar for a nightcap, and a sandwich or something for George and himself. Hapwood motioned me to hang back. "May I have a word, Mr. Berman?"

I said, "Sure. It's Mickey."

"Mickey, I wanted to have a few words with you on your own so as not to make Mrs. Higgs anxious in any way."

"Anxious about what?"

"Mr. Higgs will be telling Mrs. Higgs about me now. I'm a private detective and bodyguard. You may know since the oil spill there have been threats—phone calls, letters, emails—the usual. Are you in contact with Bill Raeburn?"

"No, not since he took off on the day of his daughter's funeral. Why?"

"Before that, did you happen to tell him about this trip: where you were going and when?"

"Well, yes, I suppose so. I don't know in how much detail. Why?"

"The day of his daughter's funeral, he turned up in the old company offices in Turtle Key looking for Mr. Higgs. Two of the secretaries saw that he had a gun in his jacket pocket. And two days ago Raeburn tried to burn down Mr. Higgs's house in New Orleans. Just to be on the safe side, I'm assuming your friend is trying to kill Mr. Higgs."

I said, "It can't be," but I didn't believe myself. Then we went in to join Roy and Anita for a nightcap.

III. Chipi Chipi

Chapter Eleven _____

RAEBURN PICKS HER UP AT NIGHT, outside of Mobile. She is fourteen, at most, a scrawny, pale white girl trying to hitch a ride with a truck at the diesel pumps. He hears the trucker say, "New Orleans, that's right, but it's against company regs. You'd have to be real nice." And the girl says, "I will be." After Raeburn pays for his gas she's still out there, the trucker saying, "Hurry up round and get in the cab, less you wanna crawl over me right now, li'l darlin."

Raeburn crosses the island and says, "I'm going through New Orleans, and you won't have to do anything." The girl looks at him and looks at his car. She's holding a straw basket tied with string. He gets in the car and she follows. The trucker calls down from his cab, "Well, fuck you, too! Hope she gives you clap!"

The girl doesn't remind him of Kate. Her hair is badly bleached to a near white. She could be a drug addict. Raeburn tells her she has to put on the safety belt. When she does, he pulls out onto Route 10. Until now, he hasn't thought of going into New Orleans.

She says, "This here's a Bonneville SSEI."

He says, "It's a Pontiac."

"I know that. Don't you know what kind? You steal this?"

"No. My name's Bill Raeburn. What's yours?" She doesn't answer. "Where are you from?"

"You know Laurel Hill?"

"No."

"Well, it's not even big as Laurel Hill. Lockhart. That's in Alabama, just over the Florida line. Near Milligan.

He says, "Is it near Pensacola?"

"No, it's thirty miles from there. And my name's Carla."

"I see." He wonders why someone so young is hitching at night. "How old are you, Carla?"

"Old enough. You want a blow job you ask straight out. Just don't get personal."

Raeburn finds it unimaginable that this girl hitchhikes around with her mouth. There is a bit of truth in the Christian News Hour he picked up when the blues station fuzzed with static north of Tampa: this girl was living in a hell. The Christian News was that the whole world is going straight to hell, but that *you* don't have to go with it because there is an insurance policy you can take out for yourself and your family in the Family of God in Heaven. And do you know who sells this policy? Raeburn had nodded. Yes, it's Lord Jesus Christ. *Jesus* is knocking on every door. There's only this one salesman, but God doesn't *need* more than one, with Jesus.

Raeburn can picture the salesman Jesus. He's walking up to the door wearing a bright brown suit and adjusting his necktie, which is a heavy manmade fiber in wide tan and brown stripes. The back of Jesus' jacket is wrinkled from where He's been sitting against one of those wooden-bead backrests on the seat of the company car. Raeburn has had this picture of the greasy Jesus all the way from Tampa to Gainesville. Gainesville is where he's bought the candy. He says, "Would you like some peanut brittle?" He rattles the bag between them. The girl's parents will be terribly worried about her. He sets down the bag and hears her pick it up. "So, Carla, how old are you?"

"Eighteen."

"Eighteen."

"Almost. In October." The brittle cracks in her mouth.

He glances at her. A misshapen crucifix hangs on her tee shirt. "What did you say you'd be in October?"

"Like I said. You have a problem with that?"

"No." No, he no longer has problems or daughters. He hears the crunch of brittle. "Does your mother make peanut brittle?"

"She makes. She makes bourbon on the rocks."

He gets it: the girl is running away from a drunken mother and, probably, a father who beats her. Kate came from a much nicer home but it hadn't saved her. Mary Ann couldn't be right about them killing Kate. Could she? There was a place near here where Mary Ann and he had once vacationed. Hotel Bellevue. He says, "Are you running away because your mother drinks? Does your father know you've gone?"

"I ain't runnin away and I ain't got a father. I mean, he's my stepfather and he's okay. My real dad died at Fort Bragg when I was little."

"I'm sorry."

"And also I ain't got no money, so I'll give you a blow job if you want."

"Please don't say that again. I don't want that. I don't want anything from you, Carla." This isn't true. He wants her to bring Kate back to life.

"Okay I won't. Anyhow, my mom don't really drink a lot. I only said that. She's okay. They're okay. It's just I hate them. Except, not really. But they're so. You know."

"So peanut brittle?"

"Yeah. I mean, what do you mean? That's weird. You're weird, you know."

She's smiling. He looks away to keep from crying. He looks out to the far point of his high beams where they're devoured by dark. He isn't exactly sure what he's going to say to Roy when he catches up with him. Something will come. He wonders if Mary Ann has gone back to Kate's grave yet. She could become like those Cuban women who are always sweeping and dusting and bringing fresh flowers to the graves. There is that funny grave-stone in Key West: I TOLD YOU I WAS SICK. Kate's stone could say: I TOLD YOU ABOUT THE OIL SLICK. This car is like a grave, all closed in, and the travel bag on the back seat with the gun in its oilskin and the new bought clothes and four hundred and eighty fifty-dollar bills of Mickey's money, after buying the car. He doesn't want this girl to be in the grave. He says, "So you're just going to New Orleans for the weekend?"

"I got a friend there. Real famous, really."

"Who would that be?"

"She's Queen Shaku-May Thibault."

"What's she queen of?"

"You don't know much, I guess. She's only *the* Voodoo Queen."

"I don't much like voodoo."

"Cause you, like, think it's all bad and with zombies and main-gauche? Well, it ain't."

"What about something else, Carla. Your folks. Cars. You like cars, right?"

"Shit, I just learn the models and stuff to sound good, you know, like with the guys?" She is silent. The wind is warm coming in the windows. It is like the dark blown in. She says, "And something else is I live with my sister cause my mom she's gone LDS, like, Mormon. The guy she lives with is a real asshole, in Tooele, Utah."

"I'm sure if your father were alive he'd look out for you. Is it okay living with your sister?"

"She's okay, sure. It's her husband Earl that's the jerk. She says 'Earl my pearl'."

"If I were your father, I'd care that you weren't happy. How old are you?"

She doesn't answer. Some minutes later she says, "Fifteen, and not next birthday, neither."

She is fifteen and running away to voodoo in New Orleans and he is forty-one and running to justify his life and his wife's life and his dead daughter's life to someone who doesn't care. Who doesn't as yet care. Raeburn sees himself as being asleep all these years. In the motel last night he'd had a bad dream. He dreamt he'd woken and gone out behind his room where his mother was kneeling at the corner of a slab, trying to lift its corner where it had sunk into the earth. She slipped a bible under it to no effect. He began handing her more bibles from a stack, but they all slipped under and the slab stayed skew. When she wanted to go to her room for more bibles, he had hit her and she sank back crouching at the slab, which was a grave. Over the stone, then, his father's head came up, his finger pointing, like Kilroy Was Here, down to the inscription: I TOLD YOU YOU WERE SICK. He'd woken with his arm burning, and he'd put toothpaste on the mosquito bites around his sores. Bad dreams. Raeburn says, "Carla, I want to tell you something: 'The sleep of reason breeds monsters.' "

"You say *what?*"

"The sleep of reason breeds monsters."

"That a put down, or what?"

"On the one hand, that really is what the sleep of reason creates. On the other, the price of eternal vigilance is freedom. Many people, not I, but many believe that freedom is not too great a price to pay for eternal vigilance. So, you can see the problem, being fatherless."

"Yeah, like you are weird is what the problem is."

Raeburn says, to the furthest point of his high beams, "I should have taught you about painting, about Goya's anti-voodoo voodoo paintings and etchings. Or baseball. I could have done at least that."

"Mister, you want a blow job?"

"No, damn it. Why do you keep asking that?"

Carla stays silent.

"I don't want you to think that every man beats his wife. Though I can't prove that. I'm going to stop for something to eat. If you're hungry I would like to buy you something to eat, and—listen carefully—I want nothing from you in return, and I do not want you to ask if I want anything. Could you bear not asking?"

She looks out the window.

A few miles on, he finds a place by a bridge, Old Dixie Diner. Carla goes off to the ladies' with her basket, saying she's going to change for New Orleans. He asks what she wants; she says anything and a Coke. He orders oyster poorboys and Cokes at the counter and asks the woman if they can eat on the creek dock out back.

She says, "You sure can, handsome, you don't mind all the Bay St. Louis skeeters eatin on your arms again. You got bit some!" She smiles and stares at Raeburn.

His forearms are lumpy with bites. The two blister bumps have swollen up.

The woman goes back with the order and returns with a spray bottle. "Here you go, handsome. You put some this on against the bites."

"Thanks."

She watches him spraying his arms. She sighs. She says, "I wouldn't do that for just anyone, cept they was as good looking as you. You look like some kind of movie star. That little girl your daughter, come in with you?"

"No. A kid hitching to New Orleans."

"And you picked her up out the kindness of your heart."

Raeburn turns away and sees Carla coming from the rest room in a very short red skirt and flimsy, unbuttoned blouse. Her lipstick is thick and uneven so that her face seems fixed in a bitter grin. She might have stepped out of a George Grosz drawing. He turns to the woman. "I'll bring it outside."

She says, "That's fine with me, you want to sit out in the dark. You're the customer."

He pays the check. Carla is over looking at titles in the jukebox.

The woman hands him his change and says, "You from Mississippi?"

"Florida."

"Florida." She leans over the counter and lowers her voice: "Tell me something? Why have all our southern men gone crazy after ten-year-old pussy? Can you explain that? Can you?"

He says nothing but leaves a ten-dollar tip for the twenty-three-dollar check. The woman leaves it on the counter and turns her back to stack dishes. When the orders come through, she gets two cokes, bags everything and sets the bags on the counter without looking at him or the tip.

They sit on the edge of the dock. Cars cross the bridge above them. He hands Carla a poorboy and Coke. They eat. She says, "It's real good. Lots of oysters and spiced up. I seen it cost ten dollars each one."

Raeburn says, "I can afford it. This is a business trip. I can put it down to expenses." He thinks of the business: he's using Mickey's money to pay Roy back.

She takes off her white high-heel shoes and dangles her feet in the water. "You seen how that woman inside there looked at me like I was some tramp and maybe you were my pimp or boyfriend?"

He says, "Never mind that." He shuts his eyes and chews. The cars on the bridge clack and hiss. In the long silences between cars is an occasional splash of fish in the creek.

"I'll tell you something, even if you get mad. I was fourteen this last May twenty-one."

"Happy birthday. Six days ago my daughter died. Our only child. She and her boyfriend. They died from choking on smoke. They were out checking the clean-up of the Coastal Oil spill out from where we live. She was seventeen."

"I'm sorry. That's real sad, mister. I forget your name."

"Bill."

"You look at this, it'd maybe help you."

Raeburn opens his eyes. Carla leans towards him, her neck chain in hand. What he's taken for a crucifix is a unicorn on its hind legs, its front legs nailed to a cross.

Raeburn nods. New age and voodoo nonsense. He wants to drop her off in New Orleans and go on his way. They finish eating in silence. When they get in the car, she says, "I been figurin on what you said, how that the sleep—no, the sleep of reason breeds monsters. I think I get it: like in a horror movie."

He turns back onto Route 10 west. If this girl had decent parents and an education, she could be like Kate. Kate's dead.

Half an hour later, she says, "We must be getting close cause the road is all bridges over the water."

"Causeways."

"Causeways."

Raeburn remembers Mickey's father saying that the problem with America was that its peasants were landless. This girl. He was a landless American peasant.

Just before midnight, he lets her off at the edge of the French Quarter. She leans over the back seat, fishes around in her basket and brings it over. "Here's this card, case you want to see the Queen. I'm sorry for you about your daughter." Her eyes are teary.

Raeburn gives her four fifty-dollar bills from his wallet. They shake hands. He sees her go to the corner and disappear. Then he knows she's taken all his money from his travel bag, when she was fishing around in the back seat. He wants to check, but he feels this would be a betrayal of the good idea of Carla he's formed. He drives off. A few blocks towards downtown, he pulls over and checks his bag. All the money is there, and he feels relieved and disloyal. He fills up with gas at an all night gas station. He thinks to buy two plastic jerrycans and fill them with gas for the long drive ahead through Texas. When he goes inside the station to pay, he suddenly buys a cigarette lighter which he knows is not for the long drive.

He drives into the Garden District and parks on Third Street, a block from Roy's house. He's seen it five years ago, on a walking tour. He'd been relieved that Roy and Anita weren't in town, so he and Mary Ann wouldn't have to make a social visit, like to a museum. Mary Ann had been disappointed. Now he walks around the corner and past the house carrying a jerrycan. He slows and sees through the gate its double galleried front that rises pale and delicately over the surrounding gardens as if making its own moonlight. He sees the crime lights on the house and on a tree in the garden. No one is on the street. He tries the gate. It opens without the lights going on, so he twists around between the iron railings and the hedge and finds the beam sensor in from the railings about fifteen inches. He presses against the railings and sidles around the front and side to the back of the house. He is two hundred feet from the back of the house. A dog could slip in as easily and set on the lights. There might also be an alarm. He steps out onto the lawn and the bright lights come on, but no alarm. He walks directly onto the porch and waits by the shuttered French windows. He doesn't have to go in. The porch is wood and the windows are wood framed and the shutters are wood and there are certainly curtains and wooden furniture

161

inside. The lights go out. He hears no alarms, no sirens. He opens the jerrycan and pours the gas along the line of windows. Plenty of fire and smoke will come from this. When the can is empty, he sets it down, checks that his hands are dry and lights the lighter. Roy won't like all this being burnt. But it is only a house, not a daughter.

He shuts the lighter and puts it in his pocket. This is Bill Rae-burn still striking out at the wrong targets. Stupid, striking out. He's not going to do this. He picks up the can and walks across the lit garden and gets back through the hedge to the fence. He waits for the light to go out and moves around against the railings to the front gate. No one is around. He walks down the empty street and around to his car and gets in. He understands that his not being seen is a miracle. There are bad miracles. This was one, but Kate's death was a worse miracle. He suddenly feels a fool to have left Mary Ann.

He drives slowly downtown where the streets are empty and the new buildings shine. He stops at a bank of phone booths. A quarter to one here; a quarter to two at home. Maybe she's stopped that craziness. He could be home in twelve hours. He calls. His voice comes on the answerphone. He hangs up and calls again. Eleanor answers. "Willy? Where are you? Mary Ann is frantic!"

"Where am I?" He looks up at the black and silver building behind him. "I'm in front of Merrill Lynch. Put Mary Ann on."

"I'll get her."

He waits for Mary Ann to come on and say that "we killed her" thing of hers. A police car passes.

"Bill? Bill, where are you?"

"New Orleans. I'm a fool."

"I've been a little crazy, too. I'm sorry."

"If I start now, I can be home tomorrow, late afternoon."

"Here? Yes. Just one thing: promise me, Bill, that you won't come home without Kate."

It is her sensible tone that takes his breath away. He takes the receiver from his ear and looks at it. Then he hangs it up quietly and goes to the car. On the seat beside him is the card. It has the name Queen Shaku-May Thibault and a Burgundy Street address.

He walks back and forth on Burgundy without being able to find the number. The air here is thick with honeysuckle, chicory, and whiskey. If he hadn't hit Mary Ann, the miracle of Kate's death would have been averted. He looks at the card, sees the arrow is a direction sign, not a magic symbol, and turns onto Barracks Street, into an unlit alley the width of two garbage cans. At its end is a storefront with two candles burning in its window. It's after one in the morning, but the sign in the door says Open. He enters and closes the door. In here, it reads Closed, but both signs, he sees, are painted on the door glass. So it's always easy to enter and impossible to leave. This is razzmatazz. It's voodoo. But he doesn't want to try the door handle. The room is empty and dark, away from the candles. He makes out a sequined voodoo flag on the back wall. Sunburst, crescent moon, steps up to a tower, a tilted crown in the flag's center. An enormous man is standing beside him. Raeburn jumps.

The man says, "We don't sell feuilles now. Come back tomorrow."

Raeburn is catching his breath. The man is well over seven feet tall. He's barechested, blue-black. His head is shaved. Raeburn says, "Carla said I should come. She gave me this card."

"Also in the day for readings. By appointment."

"I gave her a lift. My name is Bill Raeburn."

"You're that man? Are you carrying a gun or a knife?"

"No."

"Do you have twenty-five dollars for the spirits?"

"The spirits."

"The rum for the ceremony, the clairin."

"Oh, for the spirits." Raeburn gives him the money. The man motions him to follow. He opens a door and bends through.

Raeburn follows down a corridor, up a flight of stairs, and across another corridor, all old wood, dim lit, smelling of wax polish. The giant says, "When you get in the temple, stay back and don't talk."

"Who are you?"

"I serve Maitre-Carrefour. That's all."

They turn into another corridor. Raeburn is sure they're walking around a courtyard, from building to building. He hears drums. They go down a flight and through another door into another corridor. This isn't even hocus-pocus; it's security against being raided for selling liquor without a license. The drumming gets louder. The man stops, frisks Raeburn, and opens a door. Raeburn pushes into the back of a small, packed hall. He's almost at the wall, pushed into swaying by the swaying of the others' hips, legs, and elbows. He can't see Carla. Everyone he sees is black or brown.

A short woman in a white dress passes him a Jack Daniels bottle. What he drinks from it tastes like pure alcohol with a bitter cherry taste. He passes the bottle to a raised arm swaying beside him. He feels strangely comfortable. If it's hocus-pocus, it's also friendly and the drink is good. Another bottle comes his way, and he drinks from it. He can't see anyone who looks like a priestess, let alone a queen. The drumming comes from up at the front between two columns hung with flags. There is a low drum with a hollow, blood beat, and a higher drum with rolling, snapping sounds. People are chanting in a mix of Spanish and French and English, and something that could be an African language. He drinks from another passed bottle and passes it on and starts to feel his swaying. The woman immediately in front of him is swaying her head forward in deepening arcs, her arms falling forward with her hair. He unbuttons his shirt in the heat, and he drinks and wipes the sweat from his eyes, and he passes the bottle. If he can't come home without Kate, what if he brought Carla back?

"Look what I have, Mary Ann!" Like how it's a good idea to get a new puppy right away after the death of your dog. He doesn't mean Kate was a dog. Raeburn sways and claps. His father could take to this voodoo the way he does to the Church of God of Prophecy. He drinks, passes the bottle, sways faster and gets dizzy. He slows himself. The air rises yeasty. An aisle opens before him and the women in front of him. From the columns, a tall, mahogany colored woman comes slowly dancing in white skirts. Her hair is coiled up on her head, circleted in gold. She carries a stick with a silvered gourd at its end, and as she dances she shakes silver dust from the gourd. There is a split second when he thinks he sees Carla's white face moving behind one of the columns. This tall woman dancing towards him is, he knows, Shaku-May Thibault, the Voodoo Queen of New Orleans. She is before the entranced woman in front of him. The woman's head swings out wider, further forward and back, as Queen Shaku-May sprinkles her with silver. The chant is MAMBOCOMEWITHASSOFOR. MAMBOCOME WITHASSOFOR. MAMBO COME WITH ASSOFOR. Up at a column, the giant throws flames. The woman in front of him grabs her hair and pulls back her head. MAMBO COME WITH ASSOFOR. COME LEGBA MAITRE-CARREFOUR. Raeburn chants with his mouth closed. He understands what he doesn't know. COME LEGBA MAITRE-CARREFOUR. MAMBO COME WITH ASSOFOR. LOA DOWN PITEAU-MITAN. Fire shoots from the giant's mouth. Raeburn knows that trick from the oil slick. He drinks and passes the bottle. The woman in front of him drops to her knees, swinging, rolling, moaning. She shimmers under silver water. Her head falls back, eyes fixed open, mouth wide open, and she screams and rolls over dead. Raeburn knows the words: LOA DOWN PITEAU-MITAN. MAMBO COME WITH ASSOFOR. COME TONTON OGOUN. PAPA SATCHMO OGOUN.

The Voodoo Queen stands before him. She has pale blue eyes in a carved wood face. A long brown neck and the gold coiled in her coiled hair. Her voice comes: WHY YOU ENTER MY JEUNESSE.

WHAT YOU DO MY LOUPGAROU. She steps to the side and Raeburn sees Carla up at the column. He sees Carla passing into the column pale as a handkerchief. Then she reappears with her back turned toward him. Her hair is long and reddish gold. She turns her head back to him. It's Kate. Kate is there disappearing into the column and is replaced by the woman who was dead on the floor in front of him, and who now stands in a tuxedo with a red bandana on her head and a small red towel and a conch shell in either hand. Her mouth opens, smiling, big as a bag. She wipes her face with the towel and sings. MMM WHEN NA SAINTS. GO MARCHIIN IN. Louis Armstrong's voice. She goes to a woman in the crowd and blows on the conch shell. AHA HA HA! She wipes her face and kisses the woman on the mouth. OH PAPA SATCHMO OGOUN SO BAD. MMM I WAH NA BE IN NAT NUMBER. Raeburn knows the number is three, the trinity of blood and brains and spirit. He hears behind him MAMBO COME WITH ASSOFOR. He turns. Drops of cold water hit his face like silver fire. OUT OUT OUT. LEGBA MAITRE-CARREFOUR TAKE YOU BAGUI. Raeburn backs away from the Voodoo Queen who sways over him with her cold fire. He has to bring Kate back. Everyone is laughing as he sways and bumps backwards and is turned and held in the strong tuxedo arms of Louis Armstrong who kisses his mouth. MMM WHEN NA MOON. ALL TURN TO BLOOD. AHA HA HA!

He backs into a column. The giant sets him down and drinks from the oil slick bottle and puts his finger to his mouth for silence. Fire and smoke envelop Raeburn. He is Kate and Carla, Maid of Orleans, at the stake.

Three silver stars shine coldly between his eyes. They go out and he is standing up cold sober in a room. He hears the chanting and drumming one or two rooms away. The room is cool. Its floor is covered in fine, smoothed sand, and the sand is inscribed in an elaborate, continuously winding loopline. The sand reaches from the wall behind him to ten feet beyond him. Beyond that, on the wooden floor, is a semicircle of seven large earthenware jars stoppered with wide corks. In the center, back near the wall, is a chair, and on the chair are a black top hat and a pair of white gloves. They point to him. Raeburn thinks it could be a trick, yet he has never felt so clear-headed. He sees he must get the hat and gloves. But his feet are so heavy they seem anchored to the floor. Slowly he slides one foot forward and then the other. The sand grates underfoot. He has a terrible thought and turns around. The thought comes true: there are no footprints, no mark. The loop design is unbroken. He turns back. The seventh jar is uncorked. He slowly goes down onto one knee. He has to force himself down, as if he's anchored to the ceiling. He puts his hand on the sand and drags it through and sees no mark. Raeburn brings his head up slowly and sees the dirty, big bare feet beside the open jar. His eyes lift to the bruised and vein-knotted legs and to the heavy testicles hanging over the chair edge and to the beer belly and, wearing only the white gloves and black top hat, there sits his father. His voice: I'M A MORT OUT OF THIS GOVI.

Raeburn tries to imagine the trick: hypnosis, drug.

YOU MUST BE MORT TOO. SO PUSSYWHIPPED. FORGET THEM. THE DEAD DAUGHTER. THE BITCH WIFE. GET HIM. GET THAT MAN. LIKE YOU GOT ME.

Raeburn wants to clear away this obscenity on the chair. He wants to destroy it even if it's only a holograph. He says, "What must I do, Father?"

WHITE GLOVES. TOP HAT. TAP DANCE UP THE TEMPLE STEPS. DO THE OLD MAN PROUD. RIP YOUR HEART OUT.

Raeburn lunges for the chair and passes out.

He comes to in his car at dawn. The sores on his arm are bandaged. He has a vague memory of Queen Shaku-May laying leaves on his arm and binding them. He has finally met his father. Raeburn feels his father sits inside him, a violent, senseless drunk. Mary Ann, in contrast, makes sense: He can't go home without Kate.

Chapter Twelve _____

To TELL A MUSICIAN'S TRUTH, excepting Bill, what I remember most about those days in the forest is not my affair with Anita, nor Roy's jealousy, but the sound of the rain. First, last, and most, the sound and the rhythm of the mid-day rain. The locals called it "chipi chipi"—a drizzle that showed up any time after eleven and cleared off by four. I heard it come out of the sky into the high ceiba and mahogany trees, then fall to the long-John trees and down past their slim white trunks, then to the spiky palms at the edge of the plaza clearing, and from there drop and spatter on the nylon roof of my tent tight as a drum-head: pop, de-pop, de-pop-pop, chipi chipi. But that was up at Uaxactun. The rain began as we left Belize City. It was a daily feature by the time we pulled in to the visitor center at Tikal.

They all stood in that light rain, waiting: the Park Director Menendez and his assistant; the Museum Director Codina and his assistant; Captain Padrón and his NCO's with automatic rifles; and then there were assorted chefs, waitresses and waiters, and at least a dozen baggage boys. It reminded me of some aristocrat's return to the family manse in mid nineteenth century. Roy had told us he'd made a "nice" contribution to the Park and Museum and had guided Coastal Oil into making a "seriously major" donation to the Tikal Biosphere project, then in its early days. I supposed this was on the theory that you take some out and you give back—much less. This aristocratic idea came not only from the servants' line-up but also from our own swish caravan: two Landrovers and a Landrover bus carrying supplies not for thirty but for three people. Four, with George Hapwood. How could I forget our own resident goon, despite his steady refrain of "pretend I'm not here." As Anita put it, as we stepped out from our motorcade to, I promise, a round of applause: "Give Roy three hundred thousand dollars of camping equipment and a jungle-full of flunkies, and he's an absolute child of nature."

In the four or five days since Belize City, Anita had developed a good line in anti-Roy quips, for which I was the appreciative, the ideal, audience. We hadn't had a chance to be together alone on the road trip from Belize into Guatemala. Nor would we, for the next two days of feasts, toasts, and official tours. We slept in our thatched concrete huts at the lodge and met for breakfast at eight. Roy had already been out for hours to look at the hummingbirds. Hapwood was sore that he hadn't been told.

Anita said, "Why, do you like hummingbirds, George?"

"No, Mrs. Higgs."

"Call me Anita, please. We're going to be camping together for two weeks."

"Okay. No, I don't especially like hummingbirds. Or getting up before dawn, or, come to that, the heat or the rain or the bugs. But I'm being paid to protect your husband, and I'm gonna do that."

Roy said, "Of course you will, George. But not during birding hours. Two of us trying to move silently or trying to sit perfectly still will make it twice as unlikely for me spotting and photographing my little darlings. Okay?"

"Of course, Mr. ... Roy."

I said, "If you don't like the bugs, what are you going to make of the jaguars?"

Across the table of sliced fruits and rolls and pots of coffee, Captain Padrón said, "Señor, you will not see jaguars at Tikal. There are too many people here. When you are at Uaxactun, perhaps, with much luck."

I said, "Then why do the park rangers here carry rifles?"

Padrón said, "As much as anything, for to give the tourists the thrill that there might be jaguars around here."

Anita said, "Is that why you and your men carry automatic weapons: to give the tourists the thrill of thinking there may be guerrillas around here?"

Padrón, who was sitting straight, sat straighter: "Señora Higgs, our job is to defend our country. Unfortunately, there are still some people, guerrillas, yes, who would mislead and force our poor Indian population into rebellion. They are few in number, thanks to the vigilance of these rifles you have observed. But they hide in the wilder places such as the forests to the north of here and into Mexico."

We'd stopped in Flores the previous day to pick up Guatemalan money, and I'd commented on the number of armed soldiers in the bank. Roy, in a whisper, had pointed out that the bank was owned by the army. Anyway, I didn't think Padrón would like to hear what I'd observed. Roy said, "Captain, I'm sure we're all glad you're here to protect us." The last thing in my mind was that maybe Roy had requested the army be around.

In two days we trudged all the major sites at Tikal. What was trudge-like was to be in such a formal group, so continually lectured at that it seemed no single stone, let alone stele, could simply be seen and enjoyed. Roy, at one pedantic point, dropped back with me, George, and Anita, and said to her, "Sorry for all this, sweetheart. But you'll have plenty of time to poke around on your own from tomorrow, at Uaxactun. And won't that be great, Mickey?" I was still hearing Roy without irony, and I agreed it would be.

That night, I skipped the farewell cocktail party at the Museum and joined the other tourists for the trek and climb to the top of Temple Four, the highest. It certainly was different from our group: this was a real crowd. I could feel the hands of the person below on the back of my heel as I climbed the iron ladders bolted to the temple stone. The view from the top was magnificent. Everyone was quiet, watching the sun sink into the endless forest west, and all around us were the eerie sounds of howler monkeys, moving through the treetops below. It was dark night when I returned. Half a mile from the visitor center, Anita was watching for me on the path. She said, "What are we going to do at Uaxactun, darling?"

"Hapwood will be sticking to Roy, except at dawn and dusk, and Roy's already told me he's had enough ruins here to last the entire trip. We'll find a way."

We found a way. At Uaxactun we found a variety of ways. Ways came to us as fast and furiously as careless desire. Our chief way was laundry. The damp and heat made us run through change after change of clothes each day. And what was a luxurious camping trip without freshly laundered and ironed underwear? Anita and I took it to walk the mile and a half track back to the little Uaxactun park station, at the edge of the jungle village, where the station manager, Tomaso, would solemnly take the bags from us, turn around and hand them to the laundress, Marie-Angel. Roy was back in camp after his early morning hikes, sipping his fine wine and reading books on hummingbirds or crouched with camera in one of the hides he'd put up around camp by the feeders he'd hung out. Hapwood, of course, stayed at camp to be near him. Anita and I would walk about three-quarters of a mile down the track and then turn north, through yards of undergrowth that led to a small path. A quarter of a mile up this path was a ruin we'd found on our second day. It had been mapped, but was as yet unexcavated. One corbel arch was still intact, and pushing through its vines we'd found a small room, ten feet square. We cleared out the bigger vines and debris in a thrill of archeological zeal, and finding no visible painting or carving, we'd put down leaves and grasses for a different sort of thrill. We got into a routine: a walk to the temple of love, then back to the track and down to the station, where we'd exchange dirty for clean laundry, have a bite to eat, and walk back to camp without loitering.

There was another main way. Roy was a heavy sleeper, a snorer, too. Not I. Night after night, the slight rustle at my tent door woke me. I kept my eyes shut and listened as Anita came in, and I wouldn't open them until she'd positioned herself and me, whether simply lying on the floor mattress beside me or in any number of, what a book about Pompeii I remember called, "attitudes of erotic flagrancy."

And when we weren't *in flagrento*, speaking in the temple or whispering in camp, we developed our plan to set up house together. Anita wanted to leave Roy. We'd live in Coral Gables. Even New York seemed possible again in that sweet, drunken mood. And in this new household Anita would get serious about her short stories and I, gigging with top musicians, would record CD's and play jazz festivals. She even spoke of Verny and Dinny, her son and daughter of ten and eight who were at a junior dude camp in Wyoming. Could I, she wanted to know, really take to them? We were lying naked in the temple. She was holding a photo above us for me to see. I made out two blonds: plump, spoiled children. I said I knew I could. Then she said, "You're financially independent, I know, but I'm really rich. Daddy left me a trust fund—rich people aren't supposed to talk about money, but I've never minded—of a hundred and fifty million. It's mine now, not in trust, and it's worth more than that. I guess I want to know if it would make you love me less. And I'm serious."

I said, "It wouldn't make any difference: I have no plans for endowing music departments with chairs of jazz piano."

Anita said, "Not even stools?"

It's difficult to understand, now, after the afterglow, how seriously I took these daydreams. Did Anita ever believe them? Maybe, without Bill, she, as I, would have gone on together. Or maybe we daydreamed, as we made love, with the impunity of luxury.

Our camp, for example. Had our tents not been so big, had the distance between them not been so far, had, for that matter, there not been a bottle-gas-driven fridge and freezer so that our champagne could be so chilled each night, would we have gone on? Our camp was on one of the few cleared plazas so far from the main excavations back at Uaxactun village. Behind each of our tents, on three sides of the plaza, rose the low, green hills of unexcavated temples. For all I knew, the plaza could have been cleared just to give Roy a fine campsite. Then there was that most modern of, maybe the ultimate, luxury: our isolation. We came across three other people out where we were, in our entire stay, and they were two archeologists and a naturalist, all in Uaxactun professionally. If Tikal felt like someplace far from any place else, our corner of Uaxactun felt a world away from Tikal, though it was no more than fifteen miles. But all worlds have their patterns. Ours quickly developed into our middle-of-the-night love-making in our tent, then Anita leaving and our sleeping late, while Roy was out birding, then breakfasting in the "sitting room" of Anita and Roy's big two-room tent (Hapwood had already eaten and was either back in his tent or prowling the tops of the temple mounds, looking out for Roy), then sitting around when Roy returned and listening to stories like how he'd seen both the Little Hermit and the Long-tailed Hermit in this one morning, or we'd try to scare each other with safety tips like the jingle to identify coral snakes—red, yellow, black, yellow; watch out, he's a nasty fellow. Red, black, red; go on ahead. Hapwood wouldn't take part. He sat there. We sometimes asked him what he thought; he'd say he was glad we were enjoying ourselves and we should pretend he wasn't there, at which, he had enough sense to go back to his own tent and make it easier for us to pretend. Then Anita and I would go out, laundry in hand, for a little archeological walk, the one, as we said to each other, that ended with inspecting the floor and ceiling of a temple chamber. When we'd come back, mid-afternoon, we'd either go back to our tents or make plans for dinner. Roy was the chef and *sommelier* extraordinary. He was fussy and serious and produced food in that remote place almost fit to go with the staggeringly good wines he'd brought.

Come to that, despite Anita's "child of nature" joke, Roy had surprising abilities. Like the machete. The several times we did all go off trekking together, Roy led the way, which often meant clearing the path with a machete. I tried it and hacked away wildly. Roy hardly lifted the machete and let its weight take it down through his wrist. I thought it was pretty good for a pot-bellied businessman. I was with him ahead of the others, and when he stopped to wait for them, I said, "I'm impressed with how you use that."

He shrugged and wiped the sweat off his face.

"Also the way you set up the tents and camp, and the cooking from boxes and cans and jars."

He nodded.

And then I said, "You know who else would be impressed? Your father."

"You think so?"

"I'm positive."

He leaned back against a tree trunk and watched the machete as he swung it slightly between his feet. "That's one of the nicest things anyone's ever said to me." He looked down at the machete until the others joined us and we started off again.

I had no ulterior motive for the compliment. Back in that flat, endless rain forest, everything seemed to come out of the blue. I suppose it was comfortable to make myself so dumb, to imagine Roy knew nothing, to imagine, for heaven's sake, that Roy's private detective knew nothing. In retrospect, I see the ironies and double meanings for the signals they really were. Like, remembering conversations more fully. That one about the hummingbirds? Roy said to Anita, "You should get up early and come out with me. This morning I saw a Little Hermit."

She said, "Isn't that the one with the little bent surgical scissors for a beak?"

He said, "That's it." And then he said to me, "That and the Long-tailed Hermit are the only buff colored hummingbirds around here. I saw one of those today, too. Amazing, Mickey. It has a three-inch beak out from a three-inch body. How's that for well hung?"

We all laughed or smiled. A few days before, when I was taking a shower with Roy—we doubled up to save water—he'd said, "I see it's true what they say about you Jewish boys: big schnozzles, big schlongs." In other circumstances, I might have quipped back about his little snub nose. Of course, I didn't. I didn't think of this when he spoke of the hummingbird for another reason. Roy had, as we towelled ourselves, afterwards, told me of his great project. "Mickey, what do you think of when you hear the words 'The Diamond Coast'?"

"I don't know. Some place in west Africa, legacy of colonial corruption, a kleptocracy raking off the mineral profits into private Swiss accounts?"

"No, you fool. Like the Palm Coast or the Gold Coast."

"It's in Florida?"

"*Going* to be in Florida. Going to be a very classy stretch of coast with Turtle Key as its center. And it would be great if the old center of Turtle Key were part of it. I'm going to make you a very serious offer for the Samuel Berman Building, Mickey."

I took a deep breath and decided to speak my mind. "What makes you think that if Frank and I wouldn't sell you the club for all that money, that I'd sell you the place I live? Besides, it's one of the few places on the historic register, late art deco, etcetera, so you couldn't even pull it down to build your, what is it, twenty-five-storey centerpiece in glass cladding?"

"No, I want to keep it, like my father's old office building, just as it is. Mickey, this is going to be a quality, environmentally sensitive development. Why hang around to see Turtle Key in the middle of trashy, bit-by-bit strip development?"

"Roy, don't be hurt, but I put you in the same league of environmental sensitivity as, say, William Tecumseh Sherman."

"Don't I get a chance to make amends?" His voice went quiet: "Don't you think I grieve about Kate Raeburn and Bob Davis?"

I said, "I'm sure you wish none of it ever happened." I wrapped my towel around me and turned back. "Put it this way, Roy. If you offered me a hundred million, twenty times the building's value, I'd refuse you." I was on some truth high; I couldn't stop. "And I'll tell you, just this once, why. Because all that money wouldn't make me Randy Weston or Bill Evans. They're two pianists, Roy." I stepped into my sandals and went to my tent. And I immediately thought that if Roy really were developing the coast, and if I loaned Bill and Mary Ann the money to pay off their debt and mortgage, they could make a small fortune by selling TK Marine to him. Then I thought of my tough words to Roy, but I figured I had money enough to say them. Mary Ann and Bill didn't. As things stood, Roy could take TK Marine from them for nothing.

I told Anita about Roy offering to buy the Berman building.

This was late at night, after we'd all gone to bed and she'd waited and come around the plaza and into my tent and we'd made love and were lying side by side, cooled in the evaporation of our sweat. She said, "I know. Roy told me. He told me what you said. He said Bill Weston and Randy Evans. Good for you! Do you know when he first came up with the plan he wanted Groves Island to be its plush resort center? And I told him that in one of the last conversations I had with my daddy, he warned me that Roy would someday want to get his hands on Groves Island. And I told Roy I was still the senator's girl and he better not even *mention* that to me again."

I saw nothing ominous in Anita telling me that Roy confided in her. After all, I thought, we were both deceiving him. So everything went on its sexy, steamy, fine-wine way. One day Roy said he'd like to take the laundry down with Anita, for a change. He didn't mean that I shouldn't go, too, but I begged off. I didn't think I could bear him walking even part of "our way." I stuck in my tent, I read, I played my practice keyboard to the accompanying rhythms of the rain. That evening, when I turned up for pre-dinner drinks, only Roy was there. Anita had napped late, he said, and would be out soon. He poured me a Laphroaig—he had all the details right—on the ice he was so proud of, and he poured himself champagne. Krug or Roederer or Dom Perignon; he'd brought nothing less.

I said, "Where's George?"

"In his tent, I guess. Maybe we'll be lucky and he'll be very late. George is a pill, don't you think? No, that's unfair. I haven't hired him for his wit. Here's to you."

We drank.

He said, "And here's to you and Anita's secret."

"What secret?" I thought I asked very calmly.

"Why you keep taking the laundry down to the station."

Through the mosquito netting there was enough sunset left

to see the temple mound across the plaza so ancient and crumbled that I felt it would implode.

Roy said, "That place! Having lunch down at that station on that table with an oilcloth on it. Man, speak of camp! And Marie-Angel who waits table and does the laundry at the same time? Not to mention Tomaso, the *jefe,* sitting there jefeing. He asked after you, said 'Geev my esteems to Mistere Barman.' Such an unreal place could not be invented. I love it."

I was smiling, but with relief.

Roy couldn't stop. He talked on about Tomaso's clean, white, starched and ironed shirt and his filthy, crumpled trousers. He showed me a pamphlet in English translation Tomaso had given him on the local forest, which explained the giant ceiba trees as "proud cymbals of an ancient yet vibrating nation." And he liked the grilled cheese and hot pepper sandwiches, and he liked the Orange Crush and how well Anita knew the ruins around the town, and he liked how Tomaso sat at his desk fiddling with his radio and rifle and telephone, sometimes all at once. And even when he ended by saying, "I like it all, what you could call the whole laundry experience," I took it literally because, I now see, I so wanted to.

I think it was at dinner on our tenth or eleventh day up at Uaxactun that Roy decided we'd been far too unimaginative and should, next day, go on an expedition northwest, into the least-known sector of the ancient site. He spread out his University of Pennsylvania maps and we brought over our glasses of Chateau d'Yquiem—a daffy drink for that climate, but irresistible; even glum George admitting he "could get used to this stuff"—and looked where Roy pointed. Plain white, with a few dotted rectangles indicating unexcavated sites, and some of those contained question marks. And nothing except, half a foot of white away, a long dotted line on which was printed "possible boundary of Classic Period Uaxactun." Roy said, "Yes. We'll go off up in this direction. I'll even compromise and leave at eight, for you late sleepers." We though about it and sipped the wine and said yes, why not. It was Roy's holiday camp, it was Roy's wine.

I remember, just as we started the next morning, looking back at the camp and asking Roy if he thought it was safe to leave everything: we'd never all been away from camp at the same time. Roy looked at Hapwood and said, "What do you think, George; are we safe?"

Hapwood answered him: "We're safe." I thought, well, there was Captain Padrón and his men somewhere out there, and I left it at that. The first forty-five minutes walking were easy. Roy took us out on his birding route and showed us the dry-stream depression where he set up with cameras and binoculars. Then we went up a slight incline with Roy leading, from time to time using his machete and then sheathing it, as we came under the forest canopy. When we came to a mound, Roy stopped and showed us where we were. At the first two ruins, we looked around, pulled vines and grass back, and, seeing only earth and heavier vine beneath, walked on. At first the forest seemed beautiful. The smooth gray trunks of ceiba rose like stone columns between twisted strangler figs. Sometimes we could see spider monkeys moving silently up at their tops. Three yellow-beaked toucans came by like flying bananas. But after another hour or so with the ruins getting lower and lower, not really distinguishable from the undulations of the earth, except for their vague outline and Roy's pointing their position on the map, I became slightly depressed. At first I thought it was just getting tired and seeing the forest looking more and more the same. George was following Roy, then came Anita, and I was in the rear. I called for a break. Anita called up to George and Roy, and we stopped and drank from our canteens at a stone outcrop on the edge of a drop in the rock that lay under the forest floor. Anita pointed at the base of a tree by the edge; a coati with her kit behind her trotted with their long snouts down.

As we were smiling at each other, George said, "Will you look at that." He pointed down at the rock floor twenty or so feet down. At first it just seemed uniformly brownish red. Then I saw it was covered in ants. The rock floor was thirty or forty feet wide and we could see down it maybe a hundred or a hundred and twenty feet until it curved out of sight, and all of it was totally covered in ants. We all looked down at our feet. No ants were there. Roy walked off in the direction we were going. We didn't say anything. We knew what he was doing. He came back and said it was all right; they must have come from somewhere not on our path and were going away from us down there.

We started walking again. I wasn't afraid we'd come across the ants, but a real low feeling came over me. I felt I was among the dead. Dead people, a dead city, a dead civilization. We were camping among the dead. It was then I started worrying about whether I could really work harder at piano, and that led me to wonder if Anita could really work hard at short stories. And there were plump, blond Verny and Dinny to think about. I must have shown my worry, because twice Anita looked back and asked if I was okay. I said I was fine, both times. Half an hour later we came to a small clearing, across which rose a long, tree-covered slope. Roy said, "Look, we're here, just about at where the city ended, they think. Who's for going up the hill with me?"

I put up my hand and said, "Not me. I'll wait here."

Anita said, "I've about had it, too, sweetheart, until the picnic and our return trek."

Roy said, "Then I guess it's just me and you, George."

Within minutes, they'd disappeared up the slope. We sat on the roots of a big ficus tree. I was about to tell Anita about my depression, when she said, "I guess you're wondering why I'm so down."

"Why?"

"This morning Roy told me about Bill Raeburn trying to

burn down our house in New Orleans. He said you've known since Belize City. Why didn't you tell me?"

"Oh, Anita. First, I don't believe it. Second, since I don't, I didn't see the point of worrying you."

"You should believe it. There's security video showing Bill crossing our garden with a can of gasoline."

"Nobody told me that."

"He's your friend, Mickey. What's he going to do? Will he come here to… I can't even say it, it's so horrible."

I reached across and held her hand. "He isn't like that."

"When he came looking for Roy, the day of Kate's funeral, the people in the office saw he had a gun."

"I don't care what he had. He isn't like that. He would never use the gun, and he didn't actually set a fire. It's some sort of a breakdown. Anyhow, he's not suddenly going to appear here, in the middle of nowhere. He isn't out to harm Roy or you or anyone. Trust me."

"I want to. But you didn't tell me about Bill going to Roy's office with a gun, either."

"For the same reasons."

"Okay. But now that I know, you'd tell me. If you knew anything."

"Yes, of course. But I don't."

"You're sure. There's nothing else."

I thought, but I couldn't think of anything else. "There isn't."

"You haven't bankrolled this trip of his?"

"No. I did set up a line of credit to help him out. He drew it out, but I didn't know whether he gave it to Mary Ann or… How did you know?"

"Roy said Hapwood found out, from the bank."

I'd forgotten that Roy essentially owned that bank and could bend its laws pretty much as he wished. "I didn't think of it."

Anita said, "No, you wouldn't have. And you know he must be using it to hunt for Roy and you didn't tell me, Mickey."

"I see what you mean. I'm sorry. But I'm not into any plan with Bill, and he isn't 'hunting' Roy."

We sat quietly for a long time. Then we saw Roy and Hapwood coming down through the trees. I said, "Darling, we have to trust each other." And even before Anita replied, "Yes, we have to," I felt the strangeness of my words, as if ants were on my tongue.

We walked to the path to meet Roy. Anita said, "Did you find another lost city?"

Roy said, "No, but we discovered something. We made, wouldn't you say, George, quite a find."

Hapwood shrugged. "I guess so."

Roy said, "We'll tell you tonight. We'll have a discovery banquet."

I said, "A mystery."

Roy said, "Exactly. But you like mysteries, don't you, Mickey? We all do, especially when we know they'll be solved."

I said, apropos of nothing I consciously thought, "Some mysteries can't be solved. And some we wouldn't want solved."

Hapwood said, "Not too many, or I'd be out of work."

Anita said, "If there were no mysteries, George, there'd be no romance."

Hapwood gave a tight-lipped grin. "Yeah, and then I'd be out of work again."

That night Roy outdid himself. The big tent was decorated with stalks of red and yellow heliconia, and a mass of white orchids he'd found lay like a cloud as the table's centerpiece. The dinner was heated from the world's fanciest cans and jars: blinis and caviar, confitte of duck, asparagus and hearts of palm. The drink went from Roederer Crystal to Montrachet, to Richebourg with the duck and back to the Crystal, Anita's favorite, Roy said. My mood was, if anything, gloomier. I made some stupid comment about it being a nice habit, if you could get it. Hapwood was standing near me, looking out across the plaza, where our tent lamps made our tents look like big blue Japanese lanterns against the black night. He said, without turning his head my way, "People get all sorts of expensive habits. This one's not so bad."

Even I couldn't pretend that wasn't personal. I said, "Are you trying to make a special point with me, George?"

"Don't take it personally. Of course I had to find out about you in order to do my job."

"Which is…"

"Which is to protect Mr. Higgs. And, don't worry, I'll call him Roy to his face."

Then Roy said it was announcement time. Another bottle of champagne was opened. We filled our glasses. Roy took a fistful of ice and went around the table dropping a piece down the back of everyone's shirt, saying "Lighten up" each time. Typical Roy klutziness: nothing could have been heavier. I gave Anita a quick smile. She was wearing a shirt and slacks in shot silk, Tintoretto red. Bill had once told me this was Titian red with a bit of blue. I'd also heard the color called vulva blush, a bit of information I thought I'd pass on to Anita later.

Roy tapped on his glass with a knife: "Lady and gentlemen, we are gathered to honor a discovery made today at approximately eleven-fifteen in the morning, at approximately eighty-nine degrees, forty minutes west of Greenwich, and seventeen degrees, twenty-five minutes north of the equator, in block forty-six northwest of the archeological map of Uaxactun provided by the University of Pennsylvania through the Archeological Division of the Ministry of Culture of the Republic of Guatemala, in the state of El Petén."

I said, "I couldn't have put it more wittily."

Roy said, "Right. So George and I were up there, just over the crest of the hill. I was poking around with my little pick and shovel archeologist's kit, and George was… Tell them what you were doing, George."

"I was sitting on a stone."

"Sitting on a stone and I'm sizing up what covered shape to work at to see if it turns out to be a dressed stone, when George calls me. Tell them what you were doing then, George."

"I was just kicking at the ground, and I dislodged this lump of rock and earth."

"Lump the size of a softball, but more oval. So he hands it to me and I see it has a bump at one end and two smaller bumps at the other."

Anita said, "Oh, no. Wait a minute, Roy. This isn't going to be another of your bad jokes, like with that sandwich."

Roy said, "No, absolutely not. So, anyhow, I sit down and get out my Swiss Army knife and started to work away some of the earth and crud. And when I started to see what it could be, I told George and said we weren't going to tell you until I worked on it some more back here. Right, George?"

"That's right."

"And now, Anita, Mickey, George—my fellow explorers, I give you this." Roy placed a folded handkerchief in the middle of the table, by Anita's side of the white orchids. He pulled back the corners one by one. At first, because of the color, I thought it was a frog, about five inches long.

Anita said, "Oh, my God, my God!"

It was a carving in jade. It was dull with encrustation, but it was a perfectly intact crouching jaguar. Anita picked it up and held it under the lamp. Her finger traced its haunches and its wide-open mouth.

Roy said, "Some bits were too delicate for me to try to clean up, but you can see where the little lumps in its mouth will be its fangs. Well, you're the expert, sweetheart. What do we have there?"

She was looking into the jade face as if it were alive, or were the image of a god she worshipped. She closed her eyes and gently closed her hands about the carving. "Classic, Early Classic, I think."

Roy said, "When would that be?"

She opened her eyes and her hands. "Anywhere from around two-fifty to six hundred AD. I've seen something like this in the museum in Guatemala City, but not so good. And this isn't even cleaned or polished."

Roy took the carving from Anita. "Please, everyone. I want to be serious, for a minute. Anita, sweetheart, this is for you, by way of apologizing for that sandwich business, but mostly because it's rare and beautiful like you are and to say I value you and won't take you for granted."

Whatever private meanings I may have missed in his speech, I fully understood this was Roy's public announcement that he was resuming his role as loving, protective, and jealous husband.

Hapwood said, "Here, here," and lifted his glass. I didn't join him.

Anita's eyes had filmed over. She took the carving and kissed Roy. She said, "It's so fine."

In my jealousy, I became very pious. I said, "I'm sorry to spoil the fun, but unless the three of you are playing a little joke on me, you can't have that carving, Anita, because it isn't Roy's to give."

Roy said, "There's no joke, and you don't understand." He stared at me as if I were an idiot.

"But I do. That's a national treasure. You can't think you'll be allowed to keep it."

Roy said, "I knew you didn't understand. I can show this to Amalio Codina at the Museum in Tikal, to Miguel Menendez, the Park Director, even to my friend Juan de Gomez-Pena, the Minister of Culture, and be allowed to keep it. Jesus, Mickey, get real. Where do you think we are? How do you think we get to pitch our tents here and have the place to ourselves? Our good luck?"

Hapwood laughed.

Anita looked away. I felt very lonely. I said, "Is this what you think, Anita? That because you can get away with something bad, you should?"

Anita said, "Oh, Mickey."

"Aren't you afraid the Jaguar Lord will curse you for stealing him?"

Roy said, "That's pretty rich, *you* talking about stealing."

Anita said, "Roy."

Hapwood said, "You folks want me to leave?"

Roy said, "No, of course not, George. We're going to stay here and finish the champagne and go on to this 1910 Armagnac I've been saving. Just let it go, Mickey. We're going to have a swell time."

Then I lost it. I said, "Just let it go. Let the drilling go, let the oil slick go, let Kate go, let Bill and Mary Ann go, let the jaguar go and, fuck it, let's swill Roederer and loot Guatemala. Well, thanks for your hospitality, but I'm pretty tired. Good night."

But that wasn't the end of it. An hour later—I was tapping at my practice keyboard and could hear them carrying on across the plaza—a vehicle came into the plaza. Then George came around and asked me to come across. It was Captain Padrón with one of his NCO's. Two armed soldiers sat out in an army jeep. Padrón shook my hand and apologized for the disturbance. He said, "I ask you to be here together so that you may hear this directly and not, perhaps, make of it any more than it is. Today I have received information that one week ago someone who could have been this man William Raeburn was observed in southern Chiapas near the border to Guatemala. We are taking all precautions, Señor and Señora Higgs. Nevertheless, this region is heavily forest and our resources are not without limit. Should we intercept this man, whoever he may be, we will certainly treat him with respect, as you direct, Señor Higgs."

I said, "Who saw him? What did he look like?"

Captain Padrón said, "A big man, *Norteamericano*, a fair haired. As for who has seen him, Señor Berman, I may not say. There are insurgent leftists from north of here and in Chiapas, in Mexico, across the border. Some are there with insurgent Indians from Chiapas, certainly communists."

Then he excused himself, saying he had to get back down to Tikal. When he left, I said, "Before you ask, I don't know anything. *Nada*. Good night."

But it wasn't good nor was it over. I lay awake, unable to close my eyes, let alone sleep. It must have been hours later. The lights were out in the other tents. First, I thought it was a small plane, far off. Then it stopped and came again, and I thought it was thunder. The next time it came, I knew it was too low to the ground for thunder. It could have come from under my tent or from inside me. It sounded like a jaguar out there, close. Impossible even to tell what direction, and I have good ears. Then the lights came on in the other tents, and I knew Anita wouldn't visit me that night. Then I reminded myself I hadn't even been thinking of that.

Chapter Thirteen _____

I REMEMBER THE NEXT DAY being grayer than usual, but that could have been my mood. I went across the plaza to find a note saying that Anita and George had gone out early with Roy; they'd be back by ten. I made breakfast and looked at a humming-bird field guide. I couldn't concentrate. I kept imagining Bill trying to make his way through the mountains and forests, on foot. It seemed unlikely. Yet, if anyone could do it, he could. I hoped he wouldn't try. I hoped none of these reports were true. I didn't want to think about Roy in league with the Guatemalan Army, or our luxury campsite turning into an Alamo against one man. I thought of Anita, and I sipped my cold coffee surprised and un-happy that I could be jealous of Anita going off with Roy.

I was still at the table when they came back to camp all bright-eyed and jolly, the pair of them. George immediately left, as he put it, "to wash away some of this jungle crud."

Roy started making a late breakfast. Anita said, "Mickey, it was terrific. We went to Roy's hide, the one we passed yesterday, and we saw the most wonderful, tiny hummingbird: the Fork-tailed Emerald. Unbelievable, a jewel of feathers."

Roy said, "Tell him about the nest."

Anita said, "I couldn't even see it through the binoculars, but then Roy said if we were quick, we could go across and see it. And it was hanging under a leaf, no bigger than an inch and a half across, and inside were these two eggs the size of my little fingernail. Miraculous."

Roy said, "Tell him how the nest was made."

Anita said, "As if the twigs weren't delicate enough, this nest was lined with seed down and tiny grasses and lichen. It was so perfect. And, what was it, Roy, that other thing about it?"

Roy flipped eggs in the pan. "The weave: it's woven just open enough so the rain goes through it, without collecting."

I wanted to ask if they'd taken the nest and the eggs as souvenirs. I asked, "Did you hear that, last night?"

Roy said, "We heard something. Thunder."

I said, "That was a jaguar out there."

Roy said, "It could have been thunder."

I said, "Well, I couldn't sleep, and I saw your lights went on and stayed on. I figured you wouldn't do that if you thought it was just thunder."

Anita said, "No, that's right. We thought it might be a jaguar."

I said, "But not the Jaguar God sending you a message."

Roy said, "Cut it out, Mickey. Stop scaring Anita."

"Am I scaring you, Anita?"

"I don't think so." Before she looked away, I saw her eyes were jumpy.

"Am I scaring you, Roy?"

"No, nor are you much interesting me. You said your bit last night. Let's have breakfast, honey."

I said, "I'll see you later."

I didn't really see them at all, that day. I sat at my silent key-board all morning, and before lunch I bowed out from joining the three of them in driving down to the Uaxactun station. I lay around, I made some lunch, had three vodka martinis, came back to my tent, accompanied the chipi chipi with my keyboard tap-ping, and then I walked around north of the camp in the rain. I wondered if Bill were really trying to reach this place, and if he'd make it. I wondered about Charlene in Atlanta versus Anita and me in dream city. Finally, I got too soaking wet to wonder and went back to camp and changed into dry clothes. The others weren't back yet. I assumed they must have been going around the main ruins. Then I imagined that Anita had taken them, or maybe just Roy, to "our temple." Just there with Roy, would she drop hints to get him jealous so that he'd pay more attention to her, so that she'd turn him on? I didn't know how to stop thinking all this junk except to play the practice keyboard again. I tried something harder to remember—classical, Satie's "Gymno-poedies." It was good rain music. I was still at it when the sun came out, and still at it when Roy came over to ask me to join them for cocktails. I could go or I could sulk in my tent, so I went.

Anita was drinking something pink, which turned out to be a kir royale. She was wearing her dark glasses. I said hello and said I hadn't seen her in those pretty glasses for some time.

She said, "They've always been around, for when they're needed."

I said, "Anything come up this afternoon?"

Roy said, "George, tell Mickey what came up."

I was getting tired of Roy directing the others when to speak, and what to speak about.

George said, "Aside from some ruins stuff, we spent a lot of time with Tomaso on his radio set. We got patched through by Padrón to one of his men north, near the border. This guy he'd spoken to—"

"A *chiclero*," Anita said.

"Yeah, this *chiclero* guy said he'd seen someone, a gringo, moving south through the forest three days ago. Could be your pal Raeburn."

I said, "Or another gringo, or a European. That narrows it down to, what, three-quarters of a billion people? So what did you ask Padrón to do, Roy, napalm the Petén?"

Roy said, "Joke on. You can afford to. Whatever Bill has in mind, you sure as hell know *you'll* be safe. I'd have thought you would, at least, be concerned for Anita's safety and peace of mind."

I said, "Why is that?"

Roy said, "Why, as a gentleman, Mickey."

I said, "As a gentleman, I sure as hell know Anita will be safe, and you'll be safe, and George will be safe."

George said, "You can leave me out of this."

I said, "As a matter of fact, Roy, the only one I can see who really isn't safe is Bill. If that is Bill out there, and not an archeologist from Penn."

Roy said, "Hey, if it's Bill, or whoever, and he doesn't make trouble, he's got nothing to worry about, nor do you."

I said, "Alright. We can leave it at that."

Roy said, "Sure, can't we, George?"

George said, "Sure, we can."

I said, "Are you all right, Anita?"

She said, "I am. I am, really."

We sat around having too many cocktails. Then we sat around drinking too much wine with dinner. Not George. George had two beers, ate quickly, and left, saying he was going to stretch his legs around the camp. Suddenly, I figured that George had to be armed. It felt ominous how long I'd taken to think of it. So then the three of us went on drinking and talking about things to talk about; it was one of those nights when everyone was waiting for someone else to say a polite equivalent of, "This is very boring and let's call it a night." Finally, we all said, "Well," and put the dishes and glasses in to soak, and I left.

I was certain Anita wouldn't come. I fell into a deep, drunk sleep. So deep, so drunk, that Anita had to shake me awake from underneath me. I muttered that I couldn't, that I was too drunk. She proved me very wrong. We made love—I think the word is desperately. We fell asleep; I woke soon with a pain in my shoulder from my arm wrapped around her. I slid around and saw it was just before two. I woke Anita. She said, "You're right, of course, about the carved jaguar. We're going to give it to the Museum, here. Roy will make a big deal of it, but it will be where it should. It was just so heart-stopping to hold it, I couldn't think straight."

I thought maybe I'd been wrong to jump to conclusions. We kissed and held each other. I said, "If the person they've spotted is Bill, don't be afraid, Anita. He doesn't want to kill anyone. He's a good person."

Anita said, "I trust you." Then we decided she'd better get back to her tent. And that was a good decision, because about twenty minutes after she'd left, the growls of the jaguar started coming—I want to say coming up, because that's what it sounded like, as if the came up from under the earth. The lights went on in the other tents. They went off about ten or fifteen minutes later, as if George, Roy, and Anita were getting used to them or wanted to appear they were. I lay awake listening. Maybe it was three when I fell asleep.

I woke and looked at my watch: it was three-thirty. After some minutes I heard a growl. I got up and drank water against my hangover. I lay down again. Everything was still, but I knew something or someone else was in the tent before I knew how I knew. I lay still, very frightened. I smelled it, a sour, slightly rotten smell. And then I heard the whisper: "Mickey, it's Bill."

I said, "What?"

He whispered, "It's Bill. Shh. Get dressed and let's get out of here, where we can talk."

I did that. I got dressed and followed him outside, behind my tent. He said we'd have to get away from the campsite. He knew a place. So I followed him around the western temple mound, and he then continued in what seemed a straight west direction. I asked him why we couldn't stop. He said he'd explain that, too, when we stopped. After about twenty minutes he pointed ahead. He said, "Know where you are?" My eyes had adjusted to the dark, but I couldn't see anything but a slope down and a relatively treeless area. He said, "That's where Roy bird watches." I said, "How do you know?" He said, "I've been around for two days. I saw him here yesterday morning, with the others. Just ten minutes more and I'll explain."

My eyes had adjusted enough so that I saw how wild Bill looked; his face dirt-streaked, his shirt and trousers ragged and torn. I could see stained bandaging through his right shirtsleeve. The low ridge we were on became less tree-covered, and we walked west on ledges of rock. When we stopped, I made out a drop of a hundred or more feet in a series of rock shelves and ledges, to the north, and the same sort of rock formation going up from the bottom, forming a canyon.

We sat down. I said, "Are you crazy, Bill? I mean it. Have you gone crazy?"

He said, "You were wrong, Mickey. I found out I didn't just stop my father. I'm like him. Then I took off around the Gulf until I'd poured gas all over Roy's house in New Orleans and stood with a lighter in my hand ready to torch it. Then I couldn't. So then I got into this voodoo rite and hallucinated about my father, and that made me very sane. I've come down here to talk to Roy. To ask him some questions."

"Do you have a gun?"

Bill laughed. "A gun. I had a gun. My old pistol from the

193

boat. It's somewhere in the forest in Chiapas, Mexico. I traded it for a softball bat. I was in the forest with my arm getting bad, and I woke up in a guerilla camp. Nice people, local Indians. They fixed me up and I stayed and coached them in softball. I left the money for them. The bat was a trade for the gun. I figured I owed you the thirty thousand, anyway. So am I nuts?"

I touched his good arm. I said, "That's okay, Bill. That's the best use my money has been put to. But why are we all the way out here? Roy's bodyguard never leaves the camp on his own."

"It's the army. For over a week now I've known they've been after me. They patrol around here, right out to the limits of where Roy gets to. So I'm holed up, literally, in a cave about fifteen more minutes west of here. They don't go out there because there's a jaguar out there and, I guess, they're not supposed to scare it off in the reserve."

I said, "So what are you going to do?"

He said, "If Roy's on his own, early this morning, I'll speak to him. I'm not going to harm him. Later in the day, I'd better come into camp. My arm is bad. I have to get to a doctor."

I said, "But why have you come all this way? Why not just wait for Roy to get back?"

Bill thought for a while, and then he said, "Because it is all this way. I can't explain it more."

He asked me not to tell anyone he was here or where he was. When I asked why, he said, "Maybe Roy would rather not hear what I have to say." He didn't say anything more than that. He asked if I wanted him to lead me back, but I saw how exhausted he was, and I said I didn't. I think I felt more confident, feeling pretty sure he wasn't crazy and hadn't come to kill Roy. I got back to camp at about half past four and collapsed.

It was after ten when I woke up. The usual light overcast was forming overhead when I went into the living and dining area of the big tent. Roy sat at the table talking with Hapwood. Neither looked up when I came in. Roy said nothing in return to my "Good morning." Hapwood grunted. I took some coffee and sat down at the table. Hapwood told Roy he was off to his tent.

I said, "So what's the plan for today?"

Roy said, "You tell me."

"We could hunt up some ruins or maybe in early evening, we could all go and look at hummingbirds with you."

Roy said, "I didn't know you were interested."

I said, "Sure. It's just the early hours I can't take."

"Early hours for hummingbirds, you mean. You keep all sorts of early hours for other things, don't you?"

"For instance?"

"Plots to kill me, for instance."

Maybe I should have challenged Roy. But I thought I'd be better able to keep my promise to Bill by pretending ignorance. I said, "I have no idea what you mean."

He glared at me and then got up and went to the other section of the tent. I heard the buzz of his voice. Anita came out and sat beside me. Roy left the tent and walked across the plaza. I didn't like it that Anita had her dark glasses on so early. She said, "Mickey," and put her hand on mine.

I said, "Anita, what's happening here?"

"Early this morning, when Roy was out watching hummingbirds, Bill snuck up behind him and threatened him with a gun. Roy has reason to believe you saw Bill in the middle of last night. He does, Mickey, he has reason to believe Bill is going to kill him."

"Why didn't he then? If he had a gun and Roy was all alone out there, why didn't he kill him?"

"Because Bill is crazy and wants to taunt Roy, to torture him, first. He roughed Roy up this morning."

"Roy didn't look roughed up."

"I thought we were supposed to trust each other."

"You and me. We didn't promise to trust Roy."

"All right, yes, you and me. *I'm* asking you, Mickey: Did you see Bill last night?"

"Yes. He turned up about half an hour after you left. I went off with him and he told me everything. Anita, he only wanted to talk with Roy, and now he's done that. He hasn't hurt Roy and he won't. Bill's arm is badly infected and he's going to come in to camp sometime soon and we'll get him to a doctor. He's un-armed. He traded in his gun for a softball bat back in Chiapas. You know, where Padrón says he was."

"But you know where he is now."

"I know where he was, but he doesn't want me to say."

"Why?"

"Maybe because Roy has put half the Guatemalan army on his tail. It seems to me, Bill has more reason to be frightened of Roy than Roy has of Bill."

Anita put her head between her hands. I saw she was really frightened, but I wasn't sure of what. I said, "We trust each other, right? This Roy-has-reason-to-believe business. It was Hapwood, wasn't it? I've been so dumb. He must have known about us, too, and told Roy."

Anita lifted her head enough to nod. I put my arm around her. "I know this isn't how you would have chosen to tell him, but he had to know sooner or later."

She straightened and took my arm off her. "Oh, it's more complicated than that."

I said, "I'm listening."

"There isn't time now. And despite what you say, Bill tried to burn down our house. We could have been in it. The children could have. It's horrible! And he's come thousands of miles and through jungles and past police and border patrols and, yes, the army, here, trying to protect us. So it's not just Roy. I'm afraid for myself."

I started to say, "You needn't be—" but Anita pushed back her chair and ran off to her tent room. She was wrong, but I saw how she could be frightened.

I went back to my tent and unfolded the practice keyboard, but I couldn't really get into it. I kept hoping that Bill would walk into the camp and end all the nonsense I was hearing from Roy and from Anita, too. I looked out, I walked around the plaza, I went back, I played my silent songs, and when I started thinking of Bill out in his cave on those rock ledges, I'd go out again. Once, I came across Hapwood going over to Roy's tent. I said good morning. He said it was afternoon. Some time later, I made myself a sandwich for lunch but was too nervous to eat it.

The morning had dragged on forever. Then, from around two, time moved so fast that it seemed to come from some other universe. I was in my tent wondering whether I should look for Anita, when the helicopter came. A chop-chop over the rain that turned to a throbbing hurricane wind as it rocked and settled down in the middle of the plaza. I moved around it towards the main tent, where Anita, Roy, and Hapwood stood. I don't know when I noticed it was a U.S. Air Force helicopter. Maybe only after I saw this Major Albert Wilson come ducking under the rotor blades. He was followed by Captain Padrón, hugging his automatic rifle across his middle. Padrón said, "Please," indicating we should all go in. We sat around the table. Wilson said, "Hi, folks, I'm Albie Wilson," as if we were sitting around a hotel swimming pool in Miami Beach.

I said, "I didn't even know *we* were here."

Wilson said, "Just some tech support for our Guatemalan allies."

Roy said, "Thank God you are here."

Padrón did not waste time. He said, "Señor Berman, do you know where is your friend William Raeburn?"

"No."

"You have not seen him?"

I thought a little truth would buy Bill time. "Yes, I saw him last night. I know he's out there, somewhere."

Padrón said, "But you do not know where, exactly?"

"That's right."

"Because, Señor, if you could tell us, it would be a great help not only to your friends here, Señora and Señor Higgs, but also to your friend out there, William Raeburn."

I said, "I wish I could help. I can tell you he isn't armed."

Padrón said, "Because why? Because you have seen everything in his possession at where he hides?"

"No, because he said he wasn't. He's an honest man."

Padrón looked at Roy. Roy said, "I think I'm the last one here to see him: he had a gun this morning."

I said, "What kind?"

"A gun, a pistol he pulled on me and pushed me around with. Sorry, but I didn't have the opportunity to inspect its make or caliber."

Wilson said to me, "Seems like your buddy's having some sort of mental problem. Maybe the best thing would be to get him back to the States and get him some treatment."

I said, "He doesn't have a mental problem. Maybe it's Mr. Higgs who has a mental problem. My friend has an infected arm. He has no gun. He'll come here unarmed and peaceful, and then we'll get him to a doctor."

Anita said, "When will that be, Mickey?"

"Today. He didn't say what time. Maybe when he feels it's safe."

Padrón looked at Wilson. Wilson shrugged. Padrón said, "Very well. Thank you, Señora, Señors, for your time. I would ask you for today, please to not leave this area around this plaza. Thank you."

I stood. "Do I have permission to go back to my tent now,

Captain? Or do I ask you, Major? Or, really, should I say Roy?" I walked out without looking at any of them.

Ten minutes later, the helicopter revved up and then I heard it lift, circle once and go off to the south. Some time after that, when I left my tent to see if Bill, by any chance, was coming in, I saw three Guatemalan army jeeps parked in the plaza. They must have come in under the noise of the departing helicopter. They were empty. I didn't like it. How could Bill feel it was safe to come in with so many troops about? Maybe there weren't so many. I went back into my tent and shut my eyes.

It seemed only a minute later that someone was calling me. My watch said four. It was Padrón calling: "Señor Berman? A minute, please?"

I came out of the tent. Padrón was standing with Hapwood. He turned to me. "Yes, Señor, Berman. I wish once more to ask if you may now remember that you do know where is your friend, exactly?"

I said, "I don't know. Like I said."

Padrón nodded and walked off with Hapwood. I went back into my tent and lay down. I couldn't sleep. I had no idea what to do. I thought maybe if I could talk to Anita on her own, I might convince her, and she maybe could make Roy more reasonable. A few minutes later, Hapwood walked into my tent. I sat up and said, "Don't you even knock or call?"

"No, not now, Mr. Berman." He pulled a chair beside the mattress and sat down.

"What's this 'Mr. Berman' stuff, something you've picked up from Padron?"

"I'll tell you what it is. I'm not your pal or anyone's pal here. I'm a professional employed by Mr. Higgs. I'd call him Mr. Higgs except he doesn't want me to. And I'm here professionally, Mr. Berman."

I said, "Okay, do your job."

He said, "Oh, I will. I need to know where Raeburn is. You know. So tell me."

I said, "I can't because I don't know."

Hapwood took a gun from his pocket, unlocked its safety, and pushed it into the side of my head over my ear. "Mr. Berman, tell me right now or I'll blow your brains out."

It seemed so unbelievable, I just said, "No you won't. Roy wouldn't want that, nor would Anita."

Hapwood said, "You may be right about Mr. Higgs. I don't really know about Mrs. Higgs, but that isn't important because by now the helicopter should be putting her down at the airport in Flores. You are right, though, about me. If I blew your brains out, you couldn't tell me anything."

Hapwood put the gun back in his jacket, and for a moment I felt there was nothing more he could do. Then he said, "Mr. Berman, do you know what they say? If you really want to scare a pianist, threaten to break his fingers." His hand was around my wrist, his other had the fingers of my right hand bent back. I have strong hands, but they were no match for Hapwood's. I realized this at the same time I realized he'd just quoted the words I'd said to Anita, the night our romance began in the club.

I said, "Where did you pick that up?" He was starting to hurt my fingers.

He leaned down and put his face close to mine. "You stupid fuck. You think I don't know all about you and her, your trips with the laundry, that little ruined temple pigsty you fuck her in. You think I don't have photos? You think I don't have photos of the two of you fucking right here in this tent, night after fucking night? You think I didn't show them to Mr. Higgs? I'm a professional, Mr. Berman. And this is what I'm going to do. I'm going to count to ten and break one of your fingers, then count to ten again and break another. If I was a betting man, I wouldn't give you more than two broken fingers before you tell me."

My fingers were really hurting. I said, "But I don't know where Bill is."

Hapwood said, "And the stupidest fucking thing about you, Mr. Berman, is you thinking she wasn't telling her husband all about you and her and how she was jerking you off about running away with you. And now, I'm counting."

He started counting. He was pulling back on my index finger. I kept thinking he should have started with the little finger. That would have been fairer. Anita should have been fairer. She'd told Roy how Hapwood could scare me. I said all right, I'd tell him. He maybe had counted to three. I'd given up even sooner than he'd thought. I told him where Bill was, out on those rock ledges due west, near where a jaguar had its lair. I remembered everything Bill said about his location. If Bill had drawn me a map, I would have drawn it for Hapwood. I answered his questions quietly as I rubbed my index finger, and I hated myself even as I was relieved to find that there was no real damage to my hand. Then Hapwood went out to tell Padrón. I fell back onto my mattress but my good ears made out the two of them going across to Roy's tent and then a number of people running across the plaza, and then people walking off from Roy's tent, going west. So I knew before I left my tent to see Hapwood come across to me, what he'd say: that Roy, Padrón, and the soldiers were going off where I had directed them to find Bill. And I also knew before Hapwood told me that if I'd lied to him, he was going to break my fingers. The only news he had for me was that he was staying around to make sure I didn't go warn Bill, and that he knew I wouldn't stray out of his sight because if I did, he'd break my fingers.

I lay there thinking, well, Anita was terrified. That's why she told Roy. Then I thought she knew better than to be terrified and just wanted an excuse to break it off with me, because she at least could admit to herself that our little fling wasn't going anywhere. Then I tried thinking through all our days and nights together, to find what she said or did that might have shown she and Roy were playing a little game with me. All I thought was that maybe they'd done this before. She had her fling, he became jealous and interested in her again, and they lay in bed discussing what the lover had done, said he would do, was dreaming of doing but didn't have the courage, or was too spoiled or lazy to do. No matter how my thinking began, it always ended back with me: my complacency, my egotism, my blind daydreams. If I thought of Bill, then, I thought of him as an actor in my mental drama, and, at that, someone mostly offstage.

I went out to the western temple mound to watch the sunset. Hapwood, could, of course, see me. But because I was there, I was the first to see them coming back, Roy and an NCO leading and then the soldiers carrying the two wrapped bodies in two slings. I walked back down the mound and waited for them to come around. When Hapwood saw them, he said, "Why the hell didn't you say something?"

I said, "Because I'm not employed by you." I went up to Roy. I said, "He's dead, isn't he?"

Roy looked at the ground and nodded. He said, "They had to; Bill killed Captain Padrón ."

"With his gun?"

"With a softball bat. We didn't know he didn't have a gun."

"Yes, you did. I told you. What was it, Roy? What did Bill say to you that made you kill him?"

He looked up and smiled. "I didn't kill him. Sergeant Gomez, there, did."

"You killed him two weeks ago. Today was just a detail. It was your jealousy, wasn't it? Always that."

"I don't know what you're talking about."

Then he told me to get my bag packed. The rest of the campsite would be struck and shipped later. We had to take the bodies to Tikal. I glanced at the corpses wrapped in groundsheets and did what I was told.

Chapter Fourteen _____

J UST AFTER FIRST LIGHT, Raeburn watches Roy Higgs get into
position below him, at the edge of the clearing. Roy sets down
his backpack and unfolds a stool. He sits and takes out binoculars
and hangs them from his neck. He puts out a water canteen on his
left and a machete and a book on his right. He's well camouflaged
among the low palm fronds. Raeburn thinks of Roy's need to ob-
serve these very tiny birds which are so outside his ability to control. He wonders if Roy will come to see that he can't exist in the
same world as a wild hummingbird and will either leave forever or
turn the rain forest into a shopping mall.

Raeburn feels some relief from the aspirin he's taken and
thinks he'll be all right for this. He moves quietly from tree to tree
down the slope. Then he waits to cross the clearing until Roy
looks through the binoculars. Raeburn gets to a few feet behind
the stool, waits for some seconds and says, "Roy."

Roy's camouflage shirt jerks forward. He says nothing, he
doesn't turn. In the sound of Roy's gasped breaths, Raeburn sees

it would be only a matter of staying still like this for a little longer for Roy to have a heart attack and die. He walks around in front of Roy and sits on the ground. He says, "It's me, Bill." He can see the stain of pee spreading through Roy's trousers. Roy's hand is shaking. It knocks into the canteen and tips it over. Raeburn leans forward and sets it upright.

"Jesus, Jesus. Don't kill me."

"I'm not going to. I'm unarmed. See?"

Roy tries to pick up the machete but it falls from his hands. Raeburn takes the canteen and pours out a cup of water. He gives it to Roy who takes it with both hands. When he drinks, the water runs out both sides of his mouth.

"If you're not here to kill me—"

"Which I'm not."

"Why did you come?"

"To talk with you."

"All this way to talk with me."

"Mickey asked me that last night. I told him because it was all this way. I've thought about it. I think because coming all this way, I want to show you that you can't get away from what you've done."

"I'm sorry about Kate. Really, Bill, so sorry."

"No, this isn't even about Kate, or Mary Ann or me. This is about the destruction and misery you spread catching up with you. All in the name of chasing another buck. Maybe this is all the ordinary little jerks like me who you despise and step on who've come all this way to say enough is enough. Damn you, enough is enough."

"You think I see you as a little jerk? Jesus, if only. You know, it wasn't just that my father thought you were sun-up, sundown and the fucking stars at night; it was how nothing *I* ever did was good enough. Why? Because I wasn't you. President of my school debating club? Shit, that was nothing to batting five hundred.

Dean's list at Chapel Hill? That didn't mean squat compared to your baseball scholarship to Miami. Do you know that he even made fun of how I walked because it wasn't the way you walked? How I fucking *walked?* And then I take his middling business and build it into one of the biggest construction and development companies in the south, and I marry Senator Groves' beautiful daughter, and do you know what that senile sonofabitching bastard's last words were to me that I could make out? They were, and I quote: 'Love you, too, Bill boy.' Love. You. Too. *Bill*. Boy.'"

Roy is bright red and sweaty. His lips are pursed tight and his jaw juts out.

"That's too bad. I didn't have the nicest old man, either. I'm not here to trade bad dad stories. You're your own mean bastard, Roy. You build a lot of houses but you destroy more homes and lives. I'm going to do my best to fight against all that in Turtle Key, like I should have years ago. I know something, too, about being stuck in the past. I think this is what I've come all this way to tell you, here where you don't own everything in sight."

Raeburn stands. He can feel the fever coming up and knows he can move in that. But when that turns to freezing, he falls down, and he doesn't want to fall down in front of Roy.

"Where are you going? To get a gun?"

Raeburn turns back. "I have no gun. I'm going to where I'm staying, here. I won't tell you where because you'd go and somehow steal it. For what it's worth, your father was all wrong about me. I wasn't, haven't ever been worth looking up to. I never used what I was given and I never gave back."

Raeburn walks up the slope, through the trees. The cold spreads from his sore arm like it was being injected with a horse syringe of ice water. It reaches his head and his legs at the same time and he stops. Roy hasn't followed. Raeburn backs into a smooth gray tree-trunk and lets himself down against it. He tries to find an angle that will prop him up when he passes out. His shoulders hunch forward in his shivering fit. The forest blurs and darkens and he passes out.

He wakes clear-headed and weak. When he looks at his watch, Raeburn gets the rotting smell off his arm. He gets up slowly and walks west. The rain is falling when he makes his way down from the rock path to the first ledge. He holds the tree trunks for support and doubles back behind the stand of young palms and sits down at the low cave entrance. The fever comes onto his face. Flakes of fire, falling like snow. He remembers the last sunset, watching the bats rise from the caves opposite like plumes of smoke. Later, in the moonlight, the hill of limestone was veined as if milk spilled down it.

He wipes the burning sweat from his forehead. If he just walks into the camp on his own, he doesn't think Roy will have him killed. He can use the softball bat as a cane to help. He has to do this on his own. He has to clean himself. He stands and totters. The hot fever has become no different than his freezing. He crouches into the cave opening, falls down, crawls under the lintel and slowly pulls himself up by hanging his good left arm over its top. When he found the place, he thought, because of the lintel, it was an old temple. But he's decided the lintel was found someplace else and brought here fifty or a hundred or more years ago and forgotten. It supports nothing. It sits diagonally across the low entrance tunnel to the cave. His clothes are terrible. He pulls at his shirt and it rips like wet paper. He pulls the right sleeve off in slow strips so as not to rub it. The bandages beneath come off in sticky tatters and bad colors, stinking. He steps from his shoes and drops his pants and underpants and trips trying to kick them off and falls onto his left arm. Then he sits and pulls off the remnants of his socks. He tips and empties his travel bag. A clean tee shirt and a pretty clean pair of trousers. No socks or underpants, but that will be okay. He takes the foil strip of soluble aspirins from the trousers and puts all six in his mouth and chews them. They're fizzy and sharp and salty. He studies the lintel carving. Parts are white with sediment, parts are oily black. It reads left to right: the seated fat lord in jaguar skins, the servant bowing with a pronged, upright stick of office, and the bound captive with his belly to the altar. Yesterday he saw it as a bitter picture of Roy, and Roy's people, and himself. Now he sees the lord may be a composite of his father and himself, with Roy and his father thrown in for luck. And the servant is himself and the victim is Kate and Mary Ann and himself, so that he is, of course, his own victim.

He feels stronger and heady with the aspirin. He stands naked and leaves the cave and goes to the shower, a place twenty yards along the ledge where rainwater channels from the overhanging rock above. The water feels like cool silk on his hair and neck. When he gets home he will be good to Mary Ann. He holds his bad arm so that the water runs over it without hitting hard. He realizes it has stopped hurting and he wants to be pleased about this but knows it isn't a good sign. This isn't, he tells himself, the ritual cleaning of the victim. The arm won't kill him. He looks through the water across the arroyo to where he'd seen the jaguar in the last light. A red-gold movement that stopped, turned a heavy, spotted shoulder and looked back. He hadn't seen its eyes, but he remembers how he imagined them. Deep yellow and calm. Older than the carving, as old as the ledges and veined limestone. It had given a low growl and moved off. Who will believe this when he gets home? He goes back into the cave, tingling, feeling his feet aren't actually making contact with the ground. He puts on the clean tee shirt and the trousers. When he sits down to pull the shoes onto his damp feet, he falls asleep.

In his dream he's sixteen and it's the playoff game, but nothing bad has happened the day before because his parents are there, sitting together in the stands, and Mary Ann is with them, and Kate is. As he comes to the plate, he looks up into the clearest, brightest sky, and the chant begins. Hey, Billy. Hey, hey, Billy Rae.

He knows he's going to do it. Raeburn half wakes. He tries to hold to the sweet feeling. Hey, hey, Billy Rae. He is awake and there is no mother and no father and no Kate. But there is Mary Ann and a chance, her life and his, a miracle, and he knows he can do it. Hey, hey.

He props himself on his left elbow. Someone outside is calling, "Hey, Bill Raeburn. Hey, Bill." And someone else, "We know you are there, Señor Raeburn." And, "Hey, Bill, just throw out your gun. We're here to bring you back to camp." And, "Señor, throw out the gun at once and come out slowly with your hands up!"

Raeburn tries to call back, but no voice comes. His voice has burnt up. He feels for the bat and stands it vertical and pulls himself up over the fulcrum of his left hand on the handle end. A bright light pours through the entrance. They call him again. He can hear, "Hey, hey, Billy Rae." He doesn't have a chance. He has a chance, one pitch. The sun is shining in behind the pitcher. Someone in the stands lets off a firecracker, but he can stand the pain in his chest and his right arm for one pitch. The ball comes towards him, blocking out the sun, and he swings with all his might and connects and feels the solid thunk of the ball at the heart of his bat and they let off more fireworks in his chest and he falls safe at home. His eyes open and the umpire is leaning over in his camouflage uniform saying, "Qué? Qué?" What Raeburn tries to say is "Mary Ann."

Chapter Fifteen _____

THE GUATEMALAN ARMY PEOPLE had me identify Bill's body. It was thin and pale; his bloody tee shirt had all his color. His face was turned away to the side. I made myself stoop and look at it. There was no pain in his expression, not even surprise. He looked slightly worried, as if he'd been wondering if he'd done everything he was supposed to. But then, I could read into it. I told them it was Bill Raeburn. Then they had me pack and drove me from the camp in their jeep five hours to Flores. They drove hard but I didn't feel a bump. They brought me into the police station and had me sign the appropriate identification papers. I was so tired and in shock I didn't think to wonder why Roy hadn't been asked. They said there was nothing else for me to do. I could go home. They would fly the body back after the family had been notified. I asked if I might call first, *"por caridad,"* I said. I was half afraid they would decide to shoot me, too, just for the hell of it. But they made some calls and after a while handed a phone to me. It was our Major Wilson. He said of course I should call and he was real sorry it had ended bad. I remember how outraged I felt at his inability to use an adverb.

They took me to a hotel. The desk clerk said Señora and Señor Higgs and Señor Hapwood were there and would see me the next morning, that is, in a few hours. I saw it was after three in the morning. I made the call then, in one of those old telephone cubicles with an armchair and table jammed into it. The clerk dialed Mary Ann's number, and, as I hoped, Eleanor answered. She immediately asked if I'd heard from Bill.

I made a complete hash of it. I said, "Yes, I have. He turned up here to talk to Roy. And Roy had the army out because he thought Bill wanted to kill him, after this thing in New Orleans, but Bill only wanted... The point is, I'm sorry, Eleanor. I'm sorry, it's terrible. They shot him. He's dead. Bill's dead."

"Dead?"

"Yes."

She tried to catch her breath and then stopped trying and gave one gasp. I told her I'd be coming back in time to help. She said she'd let Mary Ann sleep and tell her later. She didn't know if it would register, Mary Ann was so out of it. When I asked if she wanted to know more about what happened, Eleanor said, "My brother's dead; that's about all of the story I can handle for now."

After the call, I went up to my room and fell onto the bed asleep in my clothes. The hotel woke me with a call at noon. I had to get up to go to the airport. They said the others had already left.

When I got out to the airport, I found what they meant was the others had already left Guatemala. I was told that they'd flown out mid-morning on a chartered plane. For all I know it could have been an American Air Force plane.

That was over seven years ago; I've never seen Anita or Roy since.

Back in Turtle Key, there was plenty for me to do to keep from thinking of them, and I didn't want to think of them. But, of course, I couldn't stop thinking of them. I thought of them while I made arrangements for Bill's funeral. I thought of them as I waited with the driver and hearse at Miami Airport for Bill's corpse. Eleanor wasn't there; she was taking care of Mary Ann. Mary Ann's reaction to the news of Bill's death had been silence. She moved and ate and washed and dressed as Eleanor directed, but she was mute. It was probably a mistake for us to have her at the funeral.

That was a strange event. It was a monument to inarticulateness, and I include my own sorry speech. There must have been six or seven hundred people at First Baptist Church, in the pews and isles and crammed in back and in the open doorway and down the steps and out along the sidewalks. Larry Gray, the minister, didn't say much. There was a moment, though, when his voice broke and he had to stop his conventional, understated eulogy, and I thought, yes, if he only would break down up there and just weep and all seven hundred of us would just weep, well, *that* would be honest and eloquent. But he didn't, and Mary Ann sat between Eleanor and me like a zombie and one after another, men and women came up and spoke and mumbled and stumbled saying Bill was great or wonderful in a way they couldn't put into words. To which Eleanor kept saying out the side of her mouth to me, "That's for sure," which kept my spirits up because it was funny, ironic and true, and also because I thought Bill would have appreciated it, because he was much more complex than people thought, or wanted to think. But I didn't say any of this when it was my turn to speak. I was as tongue-tied as the worst of them, though I'd written notes for my speech. But up at the pulpit, looking out over all that sadness, it came to me that I didn't want to be any different from the others in mourning Bill, not publicly, anyway. As I was about to sit down, it came into my head to say that maybe the best way we could keep Bill and Kate's memories alive would be to give time and money to keep Turtle Key from the serious over-development we all knew was under way. It could be called the Bill Raeburn Fund, or even the Stealing Home Campaign.

Then everybody went out to the North End Cemetery, the north end being one of the few places in Turtle Key high enough to dig graves without striking water. It was terribly hot and humid. People fainted with trying to stand still in that heat; only twenty or so could fit under the canopy by the grave. I don't know how many fainted, just that from time to time I'd hear a commotion and see a group fan out around someone on the ground to give her or him air. A few folding chairs were set under the canopy. Again, Eleanor and I sat as props either side of Mary Ann. Larry Gray looked at one point as if he were about to faint—which would have had him toppling into the open grave—but someone gave him water and he continued with the service. All I could think of was at least we hadn't hauled old Bob Raeburn out of his apocalyptic daydreams at the rest home for this. Eleanor decided she'd tell him afterwards, if at all.

Ritchie and Linda Martinez insisted that they host the funeral reception, the wake, I guess, since it would have been a cruel and unusual punishment for it to be at Bill and Mary Ann's home. It was a repeat of Kate's funeral, with fewer teenagers but more tears and silent drinking and looks into other peoples' eyes before looking down at your own hands or glass, as if one or the other held your soul. I remember two things about it: first, I got horribly, shit-face drunk; second, at some point, I sat down next to mute Mary Ann and she turned and said, "Don't think I don't know *exactly* what's going on," and went mute again. And I was drunk enough to think I understood her. I was sure she meant that somehow Kate's death and Bill's flight from Kate's funeral and his long chase after Roy and all the business in Uaxactun and Bill's death was some sort of male trick, a kind of irresponsible fooling around that I knew of, approved of and was totally implicated in. Of course, now I know she was crazy at that time, but I've never been able to come up with a better explanation of what she meant. I asked her when she was better. But she didn't remember saying it.

A week after Bill's funeral, Mary Ann went to Jane Rogers, outside of Tampa. That's a psychiatric institute, a hospital. She had to stay eighteen months before she could really cope.

Those were busy times for me, the first two years after Bill died. My idea for a campaign to fight the worst of Roy's plans for turning our town into a steel and plastic and concrete and golf-coursed resort caught on, and, naturally, caught me to be its first president. Successes and failures, of course. The most wonderful success was due to, of all people, Cal Joe. It turned out that he'd bought the land around his place in the late 1950's, sixty-five acres, fifty-five of which were waterfront, for a few thousand dollars, since it was mainly mangrove swamp, which he'd paid for over time. And he'd kept up paying the taxes as it was zoned as mangroves and a few agricultural acres, though the assessor's office must never have asked exactly what was being grown. And Cal Joe and his extensive, extended family set up a deal with the national wildlife people to preserve this fast-disappearing coastal land, and we—the Stealing Home Campaign—tied his shack in with the National Historic Landmark people who were delighted to get what must have been one of the last true stilt houses on the Gulf of Florida, with a lifetime tenancy for Cal Joe. And I say "of all people" because Joe and all his family had little money, and Roy was desperate for this strip, just between Groves Island and the land he owned on the coast to the north, and Joe and the Hendry's could have all been well off if they'd sold. And the example of Cal Joe and the Hendry family moved all sorts of people who had an acre here, a few acres there, to donate them so that they made up, with Joe's land, a series of natural reserves fairly ringing the town, along the coast, along the edge of the Everglades and across at the north and south, almost six hundred acres which were not, in anyone's future, going to be fucked over. And then the Sponger's Club and the Samuel Berman Building weren't selling, and Frank Edrich and I managed to convince a few other downtown owners to hold on, even though I knew more than one of them was holding on to keep ownership for when Roy's developments would make their properties worth much more than he was then offering.

On the other hand, this was America; worse, it was Florida; worse still, it was Collins County, heartland of the bubba mafia. And Roy had bought up a whole lot of land. Yet for three years, not a shovel-full of ground was broken. We were half wondering, with more hope than sense, if maybe the success of our nature-reserve scheme had discouraged him into looking elsewhere, when he held the press conference in Tampa. That's where he operated from. If he and Anita came to Turtle Key, they flew down in a seaplane and landed at Groves Island and weren't seen around town. And that press conference told me, for one, why he'd waited. He was making Groves Island the centerpiece of "The Diamond Coast," a super luxury resort with its own golf course, heliport and marina. When Terrence, the club's bartender/bouncer heard the development's name, he leaned over and said quietly—he was nothing if not diplomatic—"Mickey, that is perfection. The Diamond Coast, like the Gold Coast or the Ivory Coast, all those European names for the parts of Africa they were bleeding dry." The idea amused me, but not enough to overcome the bitterness and loneliness I felt to know that Anita had completely changed heart about her family home. I kept telling myself that I was well away from such a hard, materialistic woman. But I didn't fall for my line. There wasn't a ballad I played that I didn't think of Anita, those days and nights, those plans and promises. It did no good thinking we'd been kidding each other. Maybe that was because no one else had taken her place. I stopped seeing Ginny, and other one or two night stands. I stopped screwing around. Maybe I'd wised up, or maybe I'd just slowed down.

So down came the Senator's house and garages and swimming pool and gardens, and up went The St. James Resort. What St. James has to do with diamonds, I don't know. It was, I guess, just ritzy and exclusive sounding to Roy's corporate ear. And then the acreage to the north, the Towne Houses (where would Florida be without olde Englishe?) and developments called this Landing and that Landing, and Diamond Harbor Marine Resort and Golf Club (72 holes). And The Solitaire Beach Shoppes and the Square Cut Restaurant and Supper Club. And so forth, and all of it very big and heavy and ugly on the land, the land, I mean, which no longer was there, and the miles of bulkheaded seacoast. And Roy was horribly right in predicting that if he didn't develop it, others would and worse. Roy's development was disgusting; the others who came with him and after were whatever is substantially beyond disgusting. So here we are at the start of the new millennium looking much like all the other overbuilt, over-peopled shit heaps up and down the endless coasts of Florida which are not at all endless, which have pretty much ended, as in all over, as in toast. Except for the Turtle Key Nature Reserve system, etc. And these days someone other and younger than me heads the Stealing Home Campaign, half of whose current board never knew Bill Raeburn.

As I said, Mary Ann got better. Two years after Bill's death she took over as the club's day manager. This was no act of charity on my part. She's sharp and works hard and earns every cent of her salary.

About a year ago, I don't know why, I started thinking maybe I should see Mary Ann socially. Date her. We like each other, we get on, she's attractive. But I found I was oddly shy, as if the memory of Bill was a taboo. Then, last spring, I was invited to perform at a piano jazz festival in New Orleans, and I thought the time away from TK would give me the courage to ask her out, when I returned.

The gig was on Friday and Saturday night, and since my plane wasn't leaving until Sunday evening, I decided to spend Sunday afternoon seeing something other of New Orleans than the French Quarter. The hotel said some of the homes in the Garden District were open that weekend, so I decided to go with a group from the hotel. When we were picked up by an imitation streetcar named, of course, Desire, I thought I'd made a big mistake. But the Garden District charmed me: it was more irregular and imaginative, I thought, than its sister sections in Charleston or Savannah. We had a general description of all six houses on the tour, most named for their original owners, and as we came in to each, we were given more detailed sheets. We went into the house first, generally the ground floor rooms, followed the guide on the tour and were then ushered into the gardens where another guide walked us around and out.

It was the third house, the Tucker-La Fontaine House, where I took the detailed sheet at the door and looked at it and thought I'd leave and wait in the phony trolley. "The Tucker-La Fontaine House," it said, "the home of Mr. and Mrs. Roy Higgs II..." And then I remembered no owners had been around the other two homes. I asked the guide if the owners were at home. He said no, owners rarely stayed for open house and garden days, and he believed the owners were out of town, perhaps at their home in Georgetown. I nodded and looked down at the Roman numeral two after Roy's name and decided I was going to enjoy this. It was some house. Early nineteenth century, what would be called Federal Period, except this was decidedly French Empire: the wood, the wallpapers, the scrolled daybed, brass sphinx feet on the triple base dining table, the chandeliers, the carpets with their imperial bees. There was, I saw with some amusement, not one jot of Roy

II in Anita's house of Napoleon I. The place was wonderful; what it wasn't, was a home. It was a collection, a cold, beautiful museum, and I could almost feel sorry for Roy and understand why he wouldn't want to spend much time here.

The last room on the tour was a study, complete with ebony and mahogany desk, old oval portrait of Napoleon and, on a plinth, a wonderful alabaster bust of Josephine. The guide, a middle-aged man with a droopy white moustache and soft southern accent, reminded us to stand behind him and to please not touch anything. He gave his account of the room's chief treasures, and then the group, after a few questions, began to file out. I don't know why I lingered, maybe to try to see something I could identify with two real people I knew, one of whom, I said to myself, had been my lover. I looked again at the walls, the desk, the display cabinet with its green and gold Limoges china. Then I saw it and walked over to the cabinet.

The guide said, "Sir, please don't."

I'd missed it before because of all the green of the china.

The guide said, "I'd truly appreciate your leaving now with your tour, sir. I'd be happy to answer any question."

It had been cleaned up. In its open mouth, the fangs showed curved and pointed and perfect. The jade of the jaguar was, I saw, really an entirely different green than the china's.

The guide said, "Are you feeling all right, sir?"

I said, "I was interested in this piece. It's not Limoges."

The guide said, "No, that's a pre-Columbian carving. Mrs. Higgs is a collector, but only a few pieces are here in New Orleans. We should join the others, sir."

We joined the others. I went out and walked around the garden and imagined Bill out there starting to burn down the house. Then I left the garden and left the tour and walked and walked to keep from thinking what I was thinking. That I had everything wrong. Not just Anita: Anita was a collector. I was part of her collection, an erotic trophy that she and Roy could enjoy together, at their leisure. And not just that. Worse, that I knew nothing about character, that I was as superficial as she was. Worse, that I had, because of my shallowness and selfishness been implicated in Bill's death. Implicated? Hell, but for me he wouldn't have known where Roy was, he wouldn't have gone down there, and he wouldn't have died. All because I wanted a little fun, a little sport fucking. Mary Ann was smarter than she knew when she told me she knew *exactly* what I was up to. I'd been too busy fooling myself to understand.

I couldn't stop. A few hours later I found a cab and went back to the hotel and sat in the lobby with my suitcase and couldn't stop running this through my head, nor could I stop in the cab to the airport or on the plane or, really, to this day, though I have of course learned to live with this and am less and less shocked. There was, when I got back to Turtle Key, no way I could date Mary Ann. After everything, I think Bill Raeburn was most a hero in actually caring for someone like me.

Not, I have to say, that this has ruined my life. Far from it. My life is nice. I still like the town and the club, and I still love the music. A few years back, for instance, I went to Charlene's wedding in Atlanta. She married a real nice guy, a black guy, an ENT specialist at a big hospital. I told them whenever they came to Turtle Key to be sure to let me know, for they had a real friend in me. And I meant it.